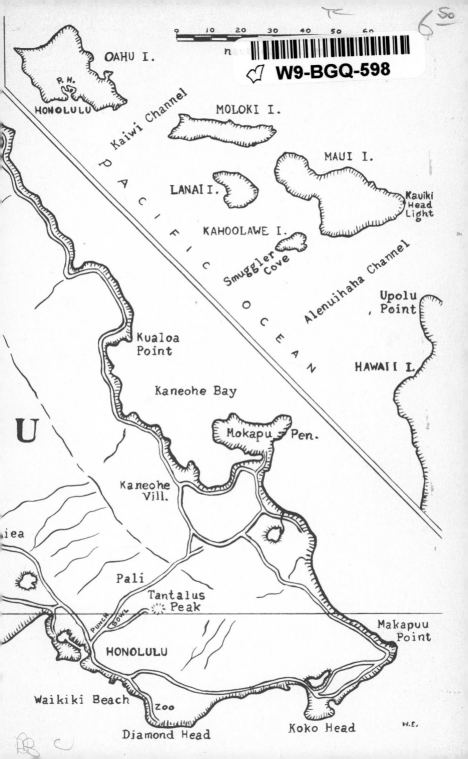

BATTLEWAGON

This is a fictional novel based upon historical fact. The USS *Nevada* did get underway during the attack on the morning of 7 December, 1941, and made a track as described in line drawing number two. However the Operations Department as related in the story did not exist on board *Nevada* at the time, but the need for such a Department became apparent to the Navy shortly after the attack and there now exists on board every warship in the naval service today an Operations Department.

As in such notable and important service novels as "From Here to Eternity," and "The Caine Mutiny" the characters and names of all principal characters are fictitious and in no way are they to be applied to persons living or dead. These character types were variously experienced in the life of the author during his twenty years in the naval service.

BATTLEWAGON

Of the Nine Battleships at
Pearl Harbor, One Got Underway

by

WALLACE LOUIS EXUM

VANTAGE PRESS

New York   Washington   Hollywood

and for JOYCE, whose
efforts and encouragement
made this book possible

AUTHOR'S NOTE

The waterfront section of San Pedro, California, especially the several blocks up from the *embarcadero*, is much like a ghost town today. Except for a few flophouses still in operation, rats, and pathetic human derelicts that walk her quiet streets and wander aimlessly around the boarded-up foyers and doorways of empty buildings that have long since been declared fire traps, this part of the town is dead. One other exception is that television companies occasionally film uninterrupted action scenes with the "good guys" chasing the "bad guys" up and down her streets and darkened alleyways.

But just over a quarter century ago this section of San Pedro was the bustling, brawling, fast, and accommodating home port of the United States Pacific Fleet. And their last Stateside home port before shifting to Pearl Harbor, two years before the infamous attack. There are some old-timers still living in and around San Pedro that would tell you, on one hand they were "sorry to see the Fleet go; but on the other hand, if they had stayed, there would be songs like 'Remember San Pedro' instead of 'Remember Pearl Harbor,' as the Japanese surely would have attacked the Pacific Fleet no matter where it was."

Be that as it may, and admitting there is little reference to the city of San Pedro in the following account, this book is dedicated to two small boys who on weekends or when school was out would thumb for rides from deep in the Los Angeles area some twenty miles northeast and go down to San Pedro for no other reason than to just mingle with the crowds of visitors around San Pedro's Fleet Landing and hoping for and often getting whaleboat or motor-launch rides out to the great battleships anchored just beyond the breakwater. There was not much notice of them, and they did behave themselves.

W.L.E.

CONTENTS

BATTLEWAGON

CHAPTER I

"WE'RE NOT RUNNING SOME KIND OF BURLESQUE SHOW HERE. THIS IS A UNITED STATES NAVY SHIP OF THE LINE!"

The bowhook sailor jumped to the finger pier and made a quick half hitch with his line to the cleat. With his rudder hard over, engines whining in reverse and churning up the clear green Pearl Harbor water into a fine salt spray, the man at the helm brought *Nevada's* motor launch snug against the sloshing rubber fenders. A pair of gleaming junior officers in starched full dress whites continued their lighthearted chatter even as they leaped from the rear of the bobbing launch to the wooden platform. Now on firmer footing, the taller of the two returned the coxun's salute and shouted, "Shove off, carry out your orders!" Then both hurried on down the Officers' landing and headed off in the direction of the vigorously playing Navy brass band.

With his bowhook back in the boat, and engines churning up the water again, the coxun began maneuvering away from the pier. He glanced down at his one passenger left.

"You think they're late for the party, Chief?" Without waiting for an answer, he continued, "Have you ever thought about how everything in this man's Navy is a 'party'? There's a shore party, a working party, an ammo party. I can think of a hundred different kinds of parties, but the best one of all is a beer party, ain't that right, Chief?"

His passenger mildly smiled back. The chief was more interested in and impressed with his immediate surrounding view than conversation.

Less than a hundred yards down from the pier and like gigantic elephants soaking up the heat of the day lay the great United States battleships *Arizona*, outboard, and *Nevada*, inboard. They were painted the normal peacetime light gray, their stately names in white block letters on their rumps. The name *Nevada* being partly obscured because of a shirtless seaman perched on a four- or five-foot length of board slung over the fantail. Directly above the seaman at each line supporting the rig were two sailors shouting down helpful hints and directions to the man who was no doubt working off some extra duty by repainting the great name of his ship—a demonstration in one of those situations that frequently comes up in any service where it takes two telling one what to do. But in spite of the good deal of white paint that had collected in the green water below him, he appeared to be doing a good job on the letters.

Nested directly ahead of the *Arizona* and *Nevada* were the *Oklahoma* and *Tennessee*, and just ahead of these the relatively newer battlewagons, *West Virginia* and *Maryland*. Not clearly visible at this point, Flagship of the Pacific Fleet, *Pennsylvania*, occupied Drydock Number One in the shipyard across the channel. On this particular weekend *California* remained at sea, on local operations with the carrier *Enterprise* and a screening force of several cruisers and destroyers. Ford Island, coming up nearly in the center of Pearl Harbor, serves the Navy as an air station. With the fleet in on weekends, this small island within an island doubles up its services with carriers, usually on the western side. And along the eastern side of the island; Battleship Row.

The coxun now clear of the pier, began threading his way back between a half dozen or so captains' gigs and an admiral's gleaming barge here and there, all laying off the

Officers' Landing waiting for instructions to come alongside when wanted. 'Like chauffeurs and their limousines double-parked around the Mark Hopkins back in San Francisco. It would be a bit chilly in San Francisco right now, but it was a scorcher here today', the chief thought to himself.

Having cleared the maze of gigs and barges, the coxun increased his speed and made a straight-on approach for the after gangway, port side of *Arizona*.

The late afternoon autumn sun was too hot for black tie and dress khakis, but it was the best uniform he had under the circumstances. Now under *Arizona*'s immense shadow it was a little cooler for the long climb up the gangway ladder and the brief formality at the top he could expect.

Enlisted men have the one seabag. Commissioned officers may have several pieces of luggage, which the messenger or stewards will care for on the double. The chief will have two pieces; seabag and footlocker, and will hope the officer of the deck will be in a good enough mood to send down the messenger of the watch, or with luck the OOD will be another chief. This chief was in better luck. The *Arizona*'s OOD was a young J.G. and apparently with some regard for CPOs. Even before the motor launch had tied up to the lower platform, the messenger of the watch was on his way down the ladder.

The passenger in the boat had one other small piece of luggage; a weather-worn eleven-by-eleven-inch-square mahogany box, about six inches deep and with a brass handle on one end. He would rather have had it tucked away in his seabag or the footlocker, but there never was enough room for it. Now, shouldering the seabag and hooking his thumb under the handle of the box, he left the boat for the platform and began the long climb up, leaving his right hand free to hold on to the side rail.

At the top, salutes and return salutes were made, and permission was granted to pass over to the *Nevada*. About thirty paces across her teakwood decks, on under her rear three 14-inch gun barrels, another salute to *Arizona*'s colors flying from her fantail, over the brow connecting the two battleships, and he was on the deck of the most important ship of his life and about a month away from one of the world's great events.

"Chief Quartermaster Earl Toland, reporting aboard for duty, sir!"

The young officer in front of Toland seemed a bit bored and late in returning his salute but did show some interest in the chief's large brown manila envelope taped to the side of his seabag that contained his transfer orders and personal records jacket of sixteen years' service. Without looking up, the short starchy officer called "Petty Officer of the Watch, log this man aboard," then reached for Toland's orders and said, in a condescending tone while leafing through his records, "You can stand easy now, Chief."

Toland let his seabag hit the deck with its full weight but hung on to his mahogany box, then turned and thanked the *Arizona*'s messenger for his assistance with the footlocker. He thought about making a comment to the young ensign in front of him about the weather, but held it.

At that moment the *Arizona*'s PA system piped "On deck, the 16 to 20 hundred watch, relieve the watch!"

Nevada's OOD looked angry, closed the chief's folder, rammed it back in the manila envelope, and said, "OK, Bosun, let's get on the ball, and pass the word!"

Turning back to Toland, he said, "You're out of uniform, Chief. Aboard this ship, whites is the uniform of the day, on weekends and after evening colors. Don't forget it! Also," he added, "I'm your Division Officer." Then he corrected himself, saying, "I'm the Assistant Division Officer for Operations."

Glancing again at the manila envelope, he seemed about to make a comment on its contents, but was stopped

4

short by a firm but soft-spoken senior officer.

"Mr. Lord! I think your relief is waiting to take the Deck." Then turning to Toland and offering his hand, "Welcome aboard, Chief. Nice to have you with us. I'm Lieutenant Commander Morgan, Command Duty Officer this weekend, but I'd damn well rather be on the beach right now. Let's get out of this hot sun," he continued, motioning toward the massive 14-inch gun turret, and saying over his right, "Bosun! Have the messenger deposit the Chief's gear in the CPO quarters, after he's properly relieved."

Morgan saw the chief casting an uneasy glance at the young officer also in the process of being relieved, and added, "Mr. Lord is going to make the Navy a fine officer someday, Chief, but right now he would rather be with the Atlantic Fleet where all the action is. I think this slow Hawaiian paradise is getting hard on him." Changing the subject, he said, "The skipper will be glad you arrived, and Operations could stand a shake up below decks, I think." He shook a cigarette out of his half-empty pack and offered one to Toland, who refused. He placed it at the corner of his mouth, lit it with a gold lighter, and said, "*Nevada* rates a Chief Quartermaster all right. We have an assigned navigator in Mr. Corbin, but he could use some assistance. He's been getting by with a First Class this past year, but Fink left us early last week, on emergency leave. I don't think he'll be coming back. The XO fired off a strong request to EPTOPAC San Francisco and, here you are. What kind of duty have you had recently?" he said, blowing smoke with the warm breeze that had just come up.

Toland clenched his jaw a little, and replied, "Recently, I just returned to active duty."

"How long were you out?" Morgan came back, still soft-spoken.

5

"Eighty-eight days, sir."

"And before that?" Morgan was looking at Toland's three ribbons; Good Conduct, China, and Phillippine Service.

"Boat captain, harbor tug—"

Toland was about to go on. He was proud of his Navy background, his last duty being skipper of his own vessel, a Hunters Point harbor tug operating in San Francisco Bay. Only a slight percentage of all Navy men, commissioned officers included, ever get command of their own vessel. And before his tug, he was the assistant navigator on two destroyers, and the assigned navigator on one old four-piper destroyer escort for sixteen months in Chinese waters. In the CPO mess and to his men on the bridge, he was no different from most other chiefs. He liked to tell stories of his experiences, from Tsingtao to Hong Kong, and up the Wang Poo to adventurous Shanghai. And he was good at it. But often he felt perhaps he got too serious with his stories, so he always found a way to end them so that his alert listeners were laughing at him as well as his tall tales. The greatest flaw in Toland's personality was that he rarely trusted anyone. He found people more reliable in groups or large organized bodies, if they were properly led, than he did as individuals. Consequently, he had made only a few lasting friends in his forty-one years of life. He wasn't happy with the apparent void between himself and others, but had simply come to live with it. However, this did not make him less valuable as a chief, and in some ways it may even have enhanced his value to the Navy. But in the past, Toland had overinstructed and he knew it. He overled and he knew that too. His past captains had often found him presumptuous and irritating, as he seemed to 'lead' them at times also. Like the time at Inchon when the captain of the old destroyer escort was experiencing the ebb of a forty-foot tide. He was unable to get his ship along the quay wall to evacuate a number of American civilians ordered out of Korea by the

U.S. State Department and the Japanese puppet government in 1934. Bow and spring lines were about to part. The captain, frustrated and angry, froze; his hands gripping the rail of the conn and turning white, as if in an attempt to 'pull' his ship in. The wall was lined with various Orientals in uniform, their laughter and mocking motions easily seen and heard on board. The executive officer, being far from on good terms with the captain, had stationed himself in the ship's office. Toland, on the bridge near his captain, knew what commands the engine and rudder needed, and he gave them, down the voice tube to the helmsman in the wheelhouse below. The ship was tied up in eight minutes, and Toland nearly got a summary court-martial for his audacity.

And it had been this same kind of audacity, this same persistence to lead, and his inability to have complete trust in anyone that was largely responsible for his failure in marriage and family. But he did try. Maybe he tried too hard. His wife didn't like the Navy, his children seemed to enjoy his being home, so he didn't reenlist after sixteen years of service. He gave up his tug command, even got a fair job at Todd Shipyard as an engineering draftsman to start. This lasted about three months. His wife filed for divorce and won it with no court appearance from Toland. And with two days to spare from the maximum ninety, he reenlisted in the Navy, still holding his present grade and with no loss in seniority. But he had lost a hunk of confidence in himself and was no nearer to really trusting anyone than he had been before. It wasn't that he disliked people. Strangely enough, he seemed to feel some kind of absurd responsibility for them.

While he might have thought of getting his tug back, he thought better of a change of duty area. Things were happening on the East Coast all right. The country was hip-deep involved in Britain's security and bound to get in deeper. But in Toland's mind he knew it was the ever widening Japanese empire that the United States would

7

have to come to grips with, and all over the whole Pacific Ocean someday. And he felt it would begin around the Philippines pretty soon.

So Toland wasn't too surprised to get orders to a ship operating out of Pearl. But a battleship. The first he would ever serve on. He had never cared for duty on anything larger than a destroyer. Common feeling prevails in the Navy—'the larger the ship, the more regulations.'

She was bound to have a commissioned officer as navigator. Toland would be the assistant navigator, he was sure.

'The *Nevada* must really need an assistant navigator pretty bad,' Toland had thought, as he pulled his gear aboard the PBY that Friday evening for the scheduled twenty-two-hour flight from Alameda to Honolulu.

And now, Saturday afternoon, November 1, 1941, and finally on board *Nevada,* he wanted to make a good impression. But at that moment, very hot, tired, and sticky, and getting a quick rundown from one of his future bosses, he remembered the relative freedom of cool afternoons on San Francisco Bay. He would have many bosses on a ship this size.

"And before that, Chief?"

"Boat captain, harbor tug, Sir."

But it was too damned hot. As Toland reached up to loosen his tie a little, he heard, then saw, a small private plane circle overhead, then come down and buzz the space between the east coast of Ford Island and the moored battleships.

Morgan noticed too, as the little plane climbed air again. He said, "One of our sister ships up ahead is having a change of command ceremony and—"

Just then *Nevada* blew tubes from her single stack, not as much as she could have, but enough to send everyone in whites cursing and scurrying for some kind of cover away from the black soot descending on them from above.

Morgan got a worried look on his face, then smiled at

Toland and motioned in the direction of the open hatch dead ahead about halfway up the port side of the main deck. The two walked hurriedly the first few feet, then ran the rest of the way. Morgan called back, "Welcome aboard, Chief!"

Inside, Morgan, catching his breath and looking himself over and at a few flakes of soot here and there on his white tunic, said, "This is one of the last split-deck wagons, but it comes in handy sometimes." He then offered his hand again, saying, "Chiefs' Mess is one deck down, halfway up the starboard side. Can't miss it. I probably won't see you again until sea detail. *Arizona* and Bat Div One will cast off tomorrow morning. Bat Div Two, that's our division, will get underway Monday morning 0800 and rendezvous five miles southeast of Maui's Kauiki Head Light at around 1600. We'll be at sea most of the week on local Ops. We generally night-steam west of Upolu Point. I would suggest you take a look at the Op order. Radio should have an extra copy. That's about it, Chief. You'll like the skipper, he's 'all Navy', as they say. See you Monday."

Toland saluted, while guessing Morgan and himself were about the same age. "Thank you, sir," the chief replied. The officer returned his salute, smiled, and then disappeared in the passageway ahead.

Now Toland was finally alone, and sighed at the relief of it. The cool air blowing through the ship helped. After tipping his hat back, he unbuttoned his khaki coat, pulled at the knot in his tie, made a space at his collar, and noticed the ladder going down at his right. After a moment more he was on his way below.

Morgan was correct, you couldn't miss it. On the door was a three-foot anchor painted in gold, with 'CPO MESS' lettered where the 'USN' usually is.

A sign hung on the handle, 'Secured'. Toland opened it anyway. Three seamen in white T-shirts and dungarees were cleaning up the painting they had obviously been doing. One came over, explaining he didn't know there would be any chiefs aboard that afternoon; those with the duty would be on call over in the *Arizona*'s CPO lounge. Toland got him to come out and show him the way to the chiefs' quarters.

Another deck down, forward, then a green felt curtain that opened into a spacious but somewhat cramped living compartment. Three bunks high all around, assorted khakis and whites hung from locker hooks. It was still a country mile better then the 'white-hat' compartments at four and five high. Some crews' compartments were still stringing hammocks, and without a square inch to spare there.

But here it was the same story as the chiefs' mess. A lot of cleaning and painting had been underway, and fresh wax on the deck. A sweaty T-shirted sailor said, "We're going to get inspected by the First Class in a few minutes, Chief, then we'll be out."

Toland smiled and said, "Sure," and asked him if he would leave his coat and wooden box near his other gear that would be in there someplace.

Having given them up, Toland dropped the green curtain, but quickly pulled it aside again and shouted to the young sailor in his teens, "See if you can locate me near a blower."

"You bet, Chief!" he came back with a grin.

There was only one thing to do now until that inspection was over. He had been thinking about it off and on since he first read his orders for the *Nevada*.

He found his way back up to the main deck where he had last parted from Lieutenant Commander Morgan. As he rounded the top of the ladder the bugler began blowing 'Mail call', then eight bells were sounded over the PA system. It was 4 P.M.

Toland stopped another young sailor and asked him the best route to the bridge. "Straight ahead, Chief. Through the mess decks, past the ship's service, on through officers' country, and five flights up. Can't miss it."

Toland pulled his tie back in place and began making his way forward up the long gray passageway. He stopped once for a drink at a frosted scuttlebutt, turned into a hatch marked 'Head', urinated, then he was on his way forward again.

Chief Toland removed his hat while passing through the crew's mess and scullery, stayed uncovered through 'officers' country' until he reached the first flight of ladders with mahogany rails all the way up. By the third flight he was beginning to feel the disadvantages of a battleship, and possibly his own age.

On reaching the fourth landing, he had two doors side by side staring back at him. The one on the left, in neat bold letters, read 'Crypto', the other, 'Radio'. Rounding the landing for the last flight up, Toland passed two more doors opposite the first two. On the left, 'Captain, Knock Before Entering'. The door to the right, 'Chart House'. On reaching the wheelhouse deck at the top of the last ladder, the bosun's pipe shrilled again, then, "*Nevada*, Returning!"

This meant the formal lawn party in front of the old BOQ on Ford Island was now breaking up. The change-of-command ceremony for one of the wagons nested ahead was over. The liberty crew would be whooping it up somewhere on King or Hotel streets in town. And the 'brass' with their gathering of family, friends, and old classmates had had enough refreshments. Probably some small talk with the big talk, of old times and new. No doubt some talk on the growing war in Europe, England's fight for her life and Moscow's and Stalingrad's resistance to Hitler's march across the Russias. And there would be some comments about Washington's pessimism over Japan and her reach for oil in French Indochina. And for those who might speculate on Japan's ability to launch a naval war against the U.S., they would have been drowned out with plenty of laughter. Some would be downright angry with those who could even suggest such a thing. But for some, a few, the thought may persist awhile.

"*Nevada*, returning," meant the captain of the United States battleship *Nevada* was spotted in his gig and now returning to his ship.

Toland was a little surprised. He expected the wheelhouse of a battleship to be larger all right. But this was more than three times the size and room he had had on his last destroyer. However, the feeling of being at the ship's 'brain' was the same.

He rested a few moments, then stepped over and dropped his hat on the top spoke of the highly polished ship's wheel, and continued to study his immediate surroundings and new place of business, taking mental note of various navigational equipment and their location. On the rear bulkheads there were panel board switches for assorted standing and running lights, and the pit log and barometer. And immediately forward of the ship's wheel was the usual 7½-inch standard magnetic compass. Toland took note of the ship's head at 225 degrees, then looked up at the helmsman's view. He noticed plenty of windows, large and square. 'One can see a helluva lot more through square windows than round portholes any day,' he thought.

Directly aft of the engine-order-telegraph on the port side of the wheelhouse was the quartermaster's desk, where various logs are kept and all pertinent events recorded while underway.

Located on the starboard side of the wheelhouse, the captain's leather bridge chair, facing forward. And behind it, the chart table, facing aft. 'Someday,' Toland guessed, 'shipwrights are going to design wheelhouses with chart tables facing forward.'

Above the table, a Chelsea deck clock ticked away passing 1620, and there were two brass voice tubes, one going to the captain's sea cabin, the other to the charthouse. And above these, a cluttered bookcase with the usual publications—*Bowditch, Duttons, Tides and Currents,*

and a copy of the *Nautical Almanac, 1941.*
Taped down on the table was a yellow and blue navigation chart of Pearl Harbor with an unerased penciled
track of *Nevada*'s last entry into port and her final approach to the Ford Island mooring posts. The track indicated rough visual fixes were made at four-minute intervals. 'Too much time between fixes,' the chief thought.

Near the upper left-hand corner of the table there lay
items of a more personal nature. He saw an ash tray
containing a half-dozen mashed-out butts, a near-empty
pack of Luckies, and writing folder belonging to one
'Brock, K.E. QM2' as indicated across the cover.

Toland felt for his pipe, then remembered it was left in
his coat, now several decks below. He turned away from
the chart table in favor of the open hatch leading onto the
starboard bridge wing. A thin layer of soot was clinging to
the decks and rails all about him.

While circling the bridge outside to the port wing, he
guessed there must be sixty to seventy warships in Pearl
that weekend. Surrounding Ford Island with her carrier
and battleship rows were tenders, auxiliaries, and patrol
craft of every class and description known to the Navy.
And over in the quiet shipyard of South East Lock and
really packed in like sardines, a dozen or so cruisers,
destroyers, and submarines—more warships in a single
port at one time than Toland had seen in all his sixteen
years' service.

"All hands stand clear of the mess decks 'till pipe down,"
came the stern voice of the bosun; then added, "Mess cooks
and the relieving watch to the head of the mess line!"

The hot sun was fast approaching the western lush
green tropical hills of Oahu. About an hour of daylight
left, Toland figured, and then remembered how beautiful
the sunsets were in the islands; wild splashes of orange,
and reds, with vivid greens and purples. Here there is very
little twilight, and night comes on swiftly.

The chief stepped back inside, retrieved his khaki hat

from the top spoke of the wheel, and was about to lay below for dinner with the crew when he heard, then saw, the figure of a ranking line officer in dress whites hurriedly climbing the ladder to the wheelhouse. The braid on his hat and shoulder boards with four gold stripes said he was a captain, and likely the captain of this ship, Toland thought, as he bit the inside of his cheek a little. The chief took a few steps back and, with hat in place, came to attention. The captain stepped in, obviously irritated, and without stopping continued on through to the starboard hatch between his chair and chart table, and on to the open bridge wing.

Preferring to be presented to the captain under different circumstances, Toland made a move for the inside ladder going down but stopped short just as the distinguished-looking gentlemen stepped back into the wheelhouse, muttering to himself and wiping his hands with a linen handkerchief. He went straight to the hand-set phone next to the panel board lights and began cranking the handle, either ignoring or unaware of Toland's presence.

"This is the Captain speaking. Get ahold of the—yes dammit, this is the Captain! I said, get the duty engineer and CDO and have them report to me on the bridge!"

He switched the knob and cranked again, then wiped his brow with his handkerchief, looked at it, and said, "Crap!" Then he spoke into the phone, "Warren, I'll be a few more minutes, you keep the girls entertained. Have the steward bring in some iced tea or something." Then, "Yes, a light snack and a rubber of bridge at your lanai later sounds fine."

Except for a voice that was a little higher than expected, and a little stoutness in the middle that could be getting support from some kind of girdle, he had the appearance and bearing one would associate with an Academy man now in command of a capital naval warship. About six feet tall, early fifties, blue gray hair on the sides, a neatly trimmed gray mustache, and a deep-tanned face with a few white sunline wrinkles. The chief remembered he once had a skipper that was so conscious of his ten-pin shape he never went ashore without a complete laceup, which required a team of stewards to do the job. With the phone now back in its socket, the captain glanced down at the few smudges on his otherwise white uniform, then looked up, straight at Toland.

"Good afternoon, sir," Toland saluted.

The captain hesitated while looking the chief up and down. He returned a casual salute, then said, "Did you see it, Chief?"

"Sir?" Toland replied.

"Did you see that newspaper plane? I'll bet he got the whole show!"

At that moment the ladder leading up to the wheelhouse began to rattle. The captain, forgetting Toland, directed his attention to it, and the chief stepped back further as Lieutenant Commander Morgan came in, followed by a younger, freckled lieutenant with a complexion that never could achieve the Hawaiian tan he would have liked.

After greetings and salutes, both lined up for the chewing out they probably expected. Looking half pained, half angry, the captain began addressing the two officers before him.

"Did either of you see that bastard flying around up there?" Without waiting for an answer he went on, "Well, I can tell you just what he saw. First, I want you to know that plane was sent over by CINCPAC's personal arrangements with the *Star Bulletin* for aerial photos of our COC party." Then sadly clasping his hands behind him, "One or two of those pictures were going to show up on the social page of the Sunday paper. Pictures the entire crew might have been proud of." Now continuing sternly, "Well, gentlemen, what photos do you suppose he got? *Nevada* smoking her pipe all over the harbor, that's what he got! Or maybe he got a picture of the Admiral and his wife

15

running for cover like the rest of us. And maybe he got a picture of those idiots hanging over the fantail. If he didn't, I'm sure the party in every gig and barge that made Officers' Landing did."

Looking directly at Morgan, the captain said, "Who was the OD on the 12 to 16?"

"Mr. Lord had the Deck, sir."

The captain frowned a moment, then said, "You will remind and instruct Mr. Lord on chapter eleven, part three, of the *Watch Officers' Guide*," and adding with some sarcasm, "I trust, even a reserve officer as yourself, is familiar with the *Watch Officers' Guide*, Mr. Morgan?"

Then, directing his attention to the younger officer, "Mr. Noel, I expect better control from the engineering spaces than what I saw today. I'll see the Chief Engineer Monday morning. You should see my wife's dress!"

Speaking to both men, in disgust, "We are running a United States Navy battleship here, not some burlesque show down town. Now shape up, dammit!"

The captain now paused for the first time. Noel responded finally with, "Aye, aye, Sir!" Morgan followed with, "Yessir." And with that the captain pushed between the two men, and went on down the ladder, barely returning their salutes.

The two men glanced at each other, then relaxed. Noel pushed his hat back, puffed up his cheeks with his own air, then said, "Maybe we should have just shot the bastard down." Morgan, now resting his left hand in his back pocket, shrugged his shoulders and made a half smile.

Neither of the two officers were aware of Toland's presence, and the chief thought it better for them if it stayed that way.

They passed some inaudible words between themselves, then turned and departed in the same direction as their skipper, leaving the chief alone in his wheelhouse. Toland remained at attention a few more long moments, with a fixed stare at the edge of the chart table.

The longest piped call in the Navy had begun over the PA system, then, "Dinner for the crew!"

Toland shook out of his blank stare and once more scanned about the room of brass tubing, windows, and wheels. Then he too departed, out through the port hatch and down the weather ladders, catching glimpses of Honolulu in the distance through *Arizona's* forward tripod mast.

CHAPTER II

"THAT'S A HELLUVA NAME
FOR A CHINESE PORT."

"Now line-handlers, man your port side! First Division, Third Section, provide!" The bosun repeated his command over the PA system as one of the CPO's, leaving his coffee behind, brushed by Toland on his way to supervise the casting off of seaward-bound *Arizona*. It was 0900 the next morning.

With only three of his fingers slightly scalded, Toland sat back down with his second cup of coffee, then proceeded to finish off his late breakfast of sausage and eggs. In spite of the sting in his left hand from the spilled hot coffee, he felt fine and refreshed after ten hours of sleep.

The evening before, Toland passed through the mess line with the crew, went below to the chiefs' quarters, and organized his gear in the locker opposite his new bunk. He showered, then very tired fell in his rack between one blanket and a clean mattress cover. He slept heavy until the sound of reveille. Then coming awake just enough to remember where he was and how he got there, he recalled he hadn't been assigned a duty section yet, so he rolled over and dozed another hour.

Toland could have slept more but Morgan's remarks about *Nevada*'s operating schedule around the Hawaiian Islands for the coming week were pressing his collecting thoughts. He figured he'd better get up and start looking over a few charts and get ahold of the Op order from the radio shack.

He showered again, shaved, and put on a clean set of khakis. While tying his black tie before the mirror, the chief decided he did look his full forty-one years, and pessimistically thought, maybe even older. The few pockmarks around his cheeks that hung on since his teens didn't bother him anymore, but they did make him look to be somewhat tougher than he really was.

His figure was good, possibly because he would rather have good bourbon than the beer most chiefs usually prefer. His short brown hair was thinning and coming on a little gray now. All in all, there wasn't anything striking that made him stand out from other men his age. A girl he once dated in high school told him he had a nice smile. That old memory would have to help now that he was single again.

About a dozen of *Nevada*'s complement of eighty-five CPOs were aboard this Sunday morning, November 2. And more than half of these were in the freshly painted chiefs' lounge and mess, and in conversation over the Sunday morning paper. Their reactions ranged from mild amusement to side-splitting merriment over the six-by-eight-inch photo in the lower right-hand corner of the second page entitled, "The Navy enjoys a Change of Command Ceremony." The polite text accompanying it read correctly the names of dignitaries attending, and the importance of a proper change of command. It did not, however, match the distinct black pall of smoke drifting down from *Nevada*'s stack and onto the crowd of people at the southeast end of Ford Island. About half the figures were stationary, including the Navy band; the rest seemed to be walking or running in directions away from the black soot.

"I'm going to clip this out and send it to my old man back in Norfolk," laughed one of the chiefs in a group at the far end of the mess table which Toland was seated. "That old salt, he'll sure get a bang out of this!"

"I'll tell ya somebody else who's gonna' get a bang out of

it, and that's this 'old man' when he sees it," said another.
"I bet he's fumin' over it right now!" answered the chief sitting closest to Toland.

At Toland's right, sunk down in an old red leather couch, a weather-beaten chief in his early fifties, and with a face that almost matched the cracked leather behind him, said in a gravel voice, "Where's Darnell! He had the fireroom duty yesterday."

"He took the first liberty boat in this morning, Pops. I saw him sneakin' around the compartment right after reveille."

Then from the group at Toland's left, "Hey, just suppose Darnell and the Chief Engineer have to come back in the same liberty boat Monday morning."

Immediately someone answered, "They sure won't be talkin' about the Army-Navy game!" and everyone laughed, including Toland. Toland's face turned a little red as he realized everyone had stopped short their laughter and was staring at him. It angered him a bit, and he felt like getting up and walking out but took another sip of his coffee instead, as one of the two mess cooks began removing his empty breakfast dishes.

"Hey, the Bears play the Packers today," one of the younger chiefs said, looking back at the sports section, "and five bucks says the Bears take 'em today, and go on to take the playoff, just like they did last year."

"Two in a row, you're full a—"

"OK, you gonna cover it or not!"

"You're on! Hey Mace, see if you can pipe that shortwave down here a little better than we've been getting it. Game's on in forty-five minutes."

"Listen, mate, you want to hear that game any better, get your ass to Chicago!"

"Atta boy, Mace, you tell 'em," said the chief bosun, coming back in from the main deck.

"Hey, Boats! How many your men did *Arizona*'s lines pull over the side this morning?" said the football fan.

"Don't knock that First Division, buddy. They're OK! You just worry about those snipes of yours. Now let me talk to this quartermaster here." The barrel-chested chief filled a fresh cup from the stainless steel urn behind Toland, then sat down next to him, his free hand held out.

"Stuckey, Chief Bosun's mate and mess president. Sorry I clipped you going out," he winked good-naturedly. "I seem to take up too much room everywhere I go."

Toland looked at the outstretched hand, then took it. And, responding to the first friendly CPO he had seen since coming aboard, returned the introduction.

"I guess we ain't a very sociable bunch around here," the bosun said. "The only traffic in chiefs we've had are the ones that either die off or retire out to pasture, and the ones we have comin' in make it off the deck."

"Now wait a minute, Boats!" said an unusually thin chief, sliding over with his coffee to join Stuckey and Toland. "Lacey came aboard here from the *Panay* three years ago, but everybody still calls him the new chief!"

Stuckey laughed, and said, "Don't get Lacey started on that *Panay* business. He'll talk your head off for an hour about it."

"Yeah, but he's not half as bad as old gunner there and his '9-turn-destroyers'!"

The old man grunted out of the red leather couch that was bolted to the deck and, with an impatient look at his antagonist, stepped over to shake Toland's hand.

Most every chief in the Navy by 1941 was familiar with both incidents: the gunboat U.S.S. *Panay*, bombed and strafed by the Japanese while up the Yangtze River in 1937, and the seven 'blind' U.S. destroyers that ran aground off Point Honda in a heavy Southern California fog in 1923.

"These young punks. They don't know what it was like in the old Navy, do they, Wheels!" the old man said, smiling at Toland, who smiled back.

"Incidentally, I'm the Pharmacist," said the thin chief, holding out his hand too. "Simpson's the name, and if these guys give you a headache, I'll give you a pill!"

"Hey, Mace! Get over here and meet your new 'Ops' Chief!" said Stuckey.

From the third table back, Chief Radioman Charlie Mace indicated he would in a moment, but wanted to finish addressing the few Thanksgiving cards he had before him. Toland was sure he knew the radioman; then he remembered.

It would have been unlikely that out of nearly a hundred CPOs aboard *Nevada* that Toland would not have had some prior acquaintance with at least one of them, from previous ships or duty stations. Relatively speaking, the United States Navy was small during the 1930s, under 100,000 in 1935. And it was not an altogether easy service organization to join. The usual requirements for acceptance were a rigid physical exam, a high school diploma, and letters of endorsement from one's schoolteachers and principal. A few remarks about the spiritual character of the candidate from his family minister was always helpful. And then you waited weeks, sometimes months, to see if you made the quota. Because of various factors, world armament and disarmament treaties, and because the country was in a deep depression, the Navy could afford to be selective. But now after the Nazi invasion of Poland and the fall of Europe, even the dreaded reserves were encouraged to reenlist.

However, before the 1929 Crash the recruiting officer wasn't so hard to get by. If you were in good physical condition, inside the age limits, and had a strong desire to get in, then that was enough in most cases.

"Toland! Earl Toland. Son of a gun!"

The two men smiled at each other across the table while shaking hands.

"Hello, Mace!"

"Hey, listen! I know this guy. We went through boots

together. Great Lakes, Illinois, 1925. He was the oldest guy in the company. Over twenty years old, and I was about the youngest. He was always pulling me out of jams." The short stocky chief radioman sat back on his bench and took a long look at his friend, and said again, "Son of a gun!"

"How've you been, Mace?" asked Toland.

"OK. Hey buddy," he said, leaning forward again, "you remember that killing we made on all that poggy bait we brought back into the company barracks? We snuck over to the canteen in the middle of the night. It was my idea though. And then the time I pissed in those yellow soap bowls when we was captain-of-the-head." Then Mace got up and began to act out the funny story. "And all those guys came in off the grinder hot and sweaty and there they were, punch'n those soap bowls and tryin' to lather up. God, did they beat the crap out of us. Remember that, Earl?"

"I remember. And I remember the lumps on my head too," answered Toland.

Mace's pantomime actions brought on laughter from the other chiefs, one of which inquired, "And who's idea was that one!"

"I don't remember, but I know I must have told that story a thousand times."

Mace sat back down in front of Toland, and the two men began going down their mental lists of duty ships and stations of the past sixteen years. The radioman had been aboard *Nevada* seven years and went from First Class to Chief three years earlier. He also indicated he was now married and had two children. His family was living right there on the island. Mace insisted Toland would have to come out to his house on their first liberty together.

"Well anyway, Earl, in case I haven't said it yet, glad to see ya aboard." Mace hesitated a moment, then seriously added, "I don't think Gonza will be so glad, but the rest of those guys in Ops will. That bastard's been king shit around here for over two years now."

Toland looked inquisitively at the other three men at the table, and Stuckey answered for Mace, "Don't worry about Gonza. There ain't nobody in this Navy senior to Quartermasters except Bosun's Mates, and Bosun's Mates don't belong in Operations, so that makes you the Division Chief, if you want it."

"Gonza's OK, I guess," said Mace. "He runs his signal bridge and everybody else in Ops pretty tight, but he could come down a peg or two."

"Hot damn, he's gonna burn up!" said the old chief gunner.

"I'd like to see his face when he finds out you're aboard," laughed the chief pharmacist mate.

"Hey, you guys! Pipe down, the game's just coming on. What do ya say, Mace? Can't you get it in any better?"

Toland followed behind his friend, down passageways and up the flight of ladders to the radio shack near the wheelhouse. Inside the noisy room of typewriters, teletype, and code signals, Mace went directly to one of the large black receivers, and after plugging in a set of earphones began carefully to adjust first one frequency dial, then another. Taking his phones off, he said, "If they want to hear anything clearer they can tune in to Harry Owens and his Royal Hawaiians." Then turning to face his three duty operators of lesser rate, "Here he is, gents! Meet our new Operations chief. He takes over tomorrow."

With an uneasy shift Toland frowned at Mace, then followed him down between the two rows of typewriters, shaking hands with one of the radiomen on the way. The other two looked up with a smile but continued copying code.

Before reaching his personal desk at the far end of the room, Mace called over his shoulder, "How about another cup of coffee, Earl?"

Toland declined the offer but made reference to his need of the Ops schedule.

"I don't need this copy," Mace said, reaching into a white folder from the second drawer down and pulling out a number of mimeographed sheets stapled together at the corner. "It's an extra copy, but you gotta sign for it."

"Sure!" answered Toland, now seated and reaching for the desk pen near an inexpensive foldout picture frame. The black-and-white photos displayed a smiling light-haired woman in her thirties with average looks, a boy not yet in his teens and with a resemblance to his mother, and a laughing five- or six-year-old girl that couldn't have had any other father but Mace.

Mace's pride was uncontainable as he saw his friend looking at the photos after signing the checkout sheet.

"Yeah, that's them! I guess they could live without me, but I sure couldn't live without them. You're the first guy I ever told that to, buddy." Toland didn't answer so he continued talking, "We met when I was going through radio school back in Diego. We were going to wait until I made third, but you know how that is. What about it Earl, you married yet?"

Toland looked up from his friend's family and answered, "No! Use to be though."

"Any children?"

"Two!"

"What happened!"

"You writin' a book or something?"

Mace looked apologetic, and said, "Sorry, buddy. Just my big nose."

Toland's face relaxed, "Ah, your nose ain't so big. The marriage just didn't work out. I wish it had, but it didn't. That's all there is to it."

"Well, you'll meet somebody else and—"

"Hey listen," Toland said while getting up, "I got to run through this schedule. See what's going on. Know what I mean?"

"Right."

Walking back between the rows of typewriters, Toland

put his hand on his friend's shoulder and said, "You look real great, buddy. I'm glad things are working out for you. And, by the way, what's this stuff about everybody in whites on the weekend?"

"Who in the hell told you that! That's just the guys in the duty section standing topside watches. Listen, *Nevada*'s a damn good ship, you'll like her. The skipper and XO are OK. But we got our share of bastards just like any other ship. The Ops officer, he's OK. A friggin' reserve, but he knows his business and an OK guy. I think the Ward Room's a little jealous of him."

Outside the radio room near the ladder going up, Mace continued talking but in a lower tone. "*Nevada*'s beginning to crawl with them friggin' reserves. Even my First Class is one. What do you think of these friggin' reserves, Earl?"

"Well," the chief quartermaster thought out loud for a moment, "we just might need them one of these days."

"Well, I don't like 'em. I don't hate 'em like some guys do, but I don't like 'em either. Gonza and Lord, they hate every one of them. Listen, Gonza's a damn good Chief Signalman I guess, but at everybody else's expense. Watch him close if you ever play poker with him. But Ensign Lord, that's the squirt you really gotta watch. He's a bastard!"

"Mace!"

"Yeah?"

"I want you to stop introducing me as the guy that's going to take over the Division. I'm not going to do it. Maybe I can help out in *Nevada*'s navigation department. I hope so, and that's all. I think I'm getting a little old, and you and me, we're going to retire in just four more years, if the world can settle its problems by then."

"Not me, buddy. I'm staying for thirty. I got to. What the hell would I do out there? I like the Navy and I know my job. Anyway, I don't want to take any unnecessary chances with my family."

"Listen, thanks for this copy. I got to look it over now. I'll see you later?"

"Right, Earl!" the chief radioman said, shaking Toland's hand once more, "and I'm sure glad you're on board," and finally adding, "say, why the hell did you get in the Navy so old for anyway?"

"Hey!" Toland answered with a smile, "Your nose really did grow since the last time I saw you."

Both men smiled at each other, then Toland headed up the one more flight to *Nevada*'s wheelhouse.

After tossing the stapled sheets on the chart table to his right, Toland took out his pipe and a small penknife and walked to the port wing of the bridge for the fresh air and another look around the harbor. The air was warm and humid and clouding up like it might rain in awhile. The surrounding mountain peaks and extinct volcano tops were not visible because of the low morning overcast.

About half the battleships that had been nested ahead of *Nevada* the evening before were no longer there, but the cage masts of the last one could be seen in the distance moving over Hospital Point, on her way to sea. In the forward corner of *Nevada*'s bridge wing a neatly dressed sailor in pressed dungarees, and in his late twenties, turned from his own gaze at the harbor to Toland. Following a courteous introduction of himself as "Brock, Quartermaster Second," he too expressed a genuine satisfaction that *Nevada* now had a chief quartermaster, and he said he was ready to assist his new chief in every way he could.

"Let me get the other guys up here. They're all on board right now anyway. Harris and Sullivan are in the charthouse, and I'll call down for Pollard. He's mess cookin', not much use to us right now, but you might as well get a look at all of us together."

Toland was about to say he would just as soon talk to Brock about the navigation equipment, charts, and publications alone, but he let him go. It was as good a time to meet the quartermaster gang as any, and for them to meet him.

Filling his clean pipe, then lighting it, Toland sat down on the stool next to the chart table and began leafing through the Op order, stopping to read paragraphs directly affecting the ship's navigational plan of operations. The middle ladder coming up from the deck below began to rattle, and the chief turned to observe two young men enter the wheelhouse. Toland could have smiled but didn't at the almost comical pair of sailors in wrinkled dungarees now standing before him. One wouldn't say they were an exact Laurel-and-Hardy pair as the larger sailor was not really fat, much bigger and taller, but not fat. While the other, about five foot six and with a good build, possessed ringlets of black curly hair forming almost a mop on top of his head that only came to his shipmate's thick shoulder. The two were obviously inseparable buddies, as they looked a little nervously at each other, then at the chief, and back at each other again.

"I'm Sullivan," the larger sailor said to Toland, cautiously holding out his hand, "and this here's the Mick!"

"Are you rated?" Toland asked, accepting the firm handshake.

"Yes, sir! We both made Third just last September."

"Ya don't say 'sir' to chiefs, Sully! What do ya think we are, still in boot camp? Anyway, they don't like it. It might identify them with them friggin' officers. Right, Chief?"

"Maybe so," answered Toland with a patient smile and continuing the long pumping handshake just offered by the shorter sailor.

"The name's Michael Harris. Me and Sully are glad you come."

"Hey, Chief!" Sullivan said, loosening up, "You know why we call him the Mick?"

"You don't have to tell the Chief, Sully. He knows my name's Michael!"

"That ain't the reason at all, Chief," continued Sullivan. "It's because he shoulda been in the movies. The whole ship calls him 'Mickey Movie Star'. Come on, Mick, give the Chief your rendition of James Cagney, like you did this morning in the chow line."

"I don't think I ought to, not right now. But listen, Chief, did ya see that movie on the fantail last night? 'The Fighting 69th', did ya see it?"

"No, I didn't."

"Too bad! That was some movie, wasn't it, Sully?" The ladder was rattling again. "The infantry, that's where all the action is. I shoulda been in the infantry, not this screwy Navy."

"Naw, Mick, you shoulda been in the movies!" answered his friend.

"You guys shoulda corrected those charts like I told ya!" said Brock, stepping into the wheelhouse again with a young boy of slender build, in white pants and T-shirt, following behind. "I see you guys introduced yourselves OK. Chief, this is Pollard. He's still a second-class seaman, but he got assigned up here a month ago on account he has a high IQ. But Chief Gonza shot him right down to mess cookin' as soon as we got him. He officially helps out up here at sea details and General Quarters only. Sometimes he comes up and lends a hand on the charts and pubs on his own. I wish we could get him up here full-time."

"How long you been in the Navy, son?" Toland asked the quiet young man, while shaking his hand.

"Almost five months, sir!"

At Toland's right a long audible sigh was released, and Mickey Harris was looking up at the overhead in disgust.

"How old are you?" Toland continued with Pollard.

"I'll be nineteen next June."

"Hey, Psycho!" Mickey said laughingly. "Tell the Chief about the Japs coming to Pearl Harbor."

An embarrassed look came over the young man's face, and after a short silence Brock explained, with a shrug,

"All the guys call Pollard 'Psycho' on account he's always reading and quoting everything he knows from the encyclopedia. Sometimes he bothers the guys. But he's a good worker though." Then turning to the short sailor, "Why don't you pipe down sometimes, Mick?"

"Well, listen!" Toland began, speaking to all four men, "Thanks for coming up. This isn't my first ship, but it is my first wagon. We'll see what happens."

The four quartermasters smiled back at their chief, then at each other, then turned for the middle ladder going down. First Mickey, then Sullivan, and Brock following behind Pollard, saying, "You guys keep the noise down going through O Country. I keep getting complaints. And Pollard, you tell the MA thanks for letting you come up." They each answered back, and Brock said once more, "Keep the noise down, dammit!"

"Brock!" called Toland. "Stick around, and let's talk some more."

In a visible conflict with himself, half wanting to talk more with his chief and the other half wishing he could avoid it, Brock stepped back in and said, after biting the inside of his cheek, "Let me get us a couple of cups of coffee first. Black OK?"

"Black's fine!"

"Black's all we got anyway."

The neatly dressed and apparently dedicated sailor was back in five minutes with two smoking thick white mugs and placed them on the edge of the chart table in front of Toland. He remarked that coffee was always brewing and available in the charthouse.

"OK, Chief! What do you want to talk about?"

"You talk first. We'll start with how many charts we're behind. Three hundred? Five hundred!"

Brock knew it was coming, but the term 'we' used by the chief instead of 'you' helped him relax. "About a thousand!" he answered, after the first sip of his coffee.

"And the publications?"

"They're all behind except those covering Hawaiian waters."

Toland knew it wasn't uncommon for a chief quartermaster or navigator to come aboard a new ship and find the charts and pub corrections several Notice-to-Mariners behind, but this much was more than twice the number he had expected.

Toland thought a moment, then said, "We'll start concentration on all Pacific Islands north of the Equator, including the Philippines. We'll bring those charts up to date and keep card notices on the rest. The card file will include the Atlantic and Pacific seaboards, as well as European and Mediterranean waters. How does that sound?"

"Sweet Jesus, I guess! I've been trying for over a year now to get a card file going instead of correcting all these damn charts. I'm up to my ass in them right now. You know what portfolio I've been trying to bring up this month? The Baltic! And here we are way out in the middle of the Pacific. It don't make sense. But Listen, Chief, you'll still have to talk to Mr. Corbin."

"I'll talk to him. Now what about 'Laurel and Hardy' there, and this other kid we have. How come you're all aboard! You under restriction or something?"

"Glad you brought that up, Chief. Very glad you brought that up." Brock shook out a cigarette and offered one to Toland who refused, then put one in his mouth and lit it, and pulled over an ash tray made from an expended 5-inch shell base. "Yes, sir, very glad you brought that up. Do you know we got the sharpest-looking signal bridge in the fleet? And granted, I understand they are pretty sharp operators up there too. When it comes to flag hoist and tactical maneuvers, well, we always seem to know where we are in the formation, but we don't always know where we are on the globe."

"All right, Brock, just tell me what the situation is, why we got a thousand charts behind in upkeep." Then holding up his hand, Toland took a sip of his hot coffee then continued, "Just because *Nevada*'s got a good signal bridge and keeps us from ramming other ships in the fleet doesn't mean we got to have a slack navigation section. We're not in any way competing with the signal bridge."

"OK, OK! This is it. I'm a compartment PO right now. Gonza has got me—Chief Gonza put me down there twice this year already, and three months at a clip. Sully and the Mick, well they're pretty good guys and they can put out some good work, but they gotta have some supervision or they'll foul up all over the place and keep getting in trouble. Well, Fink—honest to God that was his name, Fink!—well, Fink, he couldn't handle himself even if he was all alone in the head. How he ever made First Class I'll never know. Anyway, Chief Gonza had him buffaloed. But not enough that he didn't know that the chartroom was so far behind it might not ever get caught up. He might even lose his rate. That's why he went on that emergency leave. I'd bet on it. Anyway, just let me get these guys goin' on a program and Ensign Lord comes along and motors them up to this wheelhouse to spend the day shining this damn brass work and maybe do a little painting, then he gets compliments for it from the 'old man' because the wheelhouse looks so good. Ensign Lord's responsible to see that all of Operations' spaces are clean and maintenance-free, that's his job."

So far Toland wasn't overly impressed with his second class quartermaster's aches and pains. They were of the common variety found on board any ship any day of the week. But every man on a ship has to let off steam once in a while. If anything, he thought, it might be doing Brock some good. However, Brock's next remarks gave the chief a little more to be concerned about.

"Now you asked about the liberty and why the QM's are all aboard today. Here it is the weekend, and they're all aboard!"

"When's pay-call for *Nevada*?" Toland interrupted.

"Every other Monday," Brock answered, reaching up over the chart table and sliding back several books to reveal a taped-up calendar for the year 1941. There, beneath the shapely figure of a girl drawn by Varga were ten months of the year crossed out, leaving November and December. The Mondays, 10th and 24th of November, were circled in red, as were the Mondays 8th and 22nd of December.

"Next pay-call is the 10th of November, and here it is the second. These guys are broke already. I'm not, but they are. And not just a week after pay-call either. They're always broke!"

"What's your duty section?"

"One! I got the duty this weekend. The ship's running five sections. Sully's in two, the Mick's three, Pollard should be in four, and Fink was in five."

"OK, Brock, what's your answer?" Toland asked, taking another sip of his coffee. "An all-night crap game up in the focs'l every other Monday? Or maybe Sully and the Mick are saltin' away a little security with their mothers, or girlfriends back home."

"That ain't it. It's Gonza!"

"That's Chief Gonza to you, buddy," Toland said smoothly.

"OK! Chief Gonza to me. But Chief Bastard to a lot of other guys just the same. Between his whores in Pearl City and his slush fund on here he has most of the Operations' gang and their money wrapped up in his hip pocket every other Monday."

"But not you!"

"Hell no, not me! I warned these guys over a year ago back in Long Beach not to get tied up with him. You know what his rate is? It's three for two! I've seen and been in a lot of slush funds before, at eleven for ten bucks, even six for five, but never three for two. That's robbery, and you know it, Chief."

"That's pretty strong all right," Toland answered, with

a half smile, "but nobody forces anybody into a slush fund."

"I didn't say they were forced in!" Then with a shrug Brock added, "But out here they were just stupid, and got in deeper and deeper. If we were Stateside they could'a found all the broads they wanted. It's Gonza's whores that did it."

"Well, with these guys on board all the time it seems to me you could get a lot of work out of them."

"I thought I explained all that. Listen, Chief. Forget it!" said Brock almost snapping back, "Welcome aboard, and all that good stuff. If there aren't any more questions," he continued, downing the rest of his coffee and reaching for Toland's cup, "then I got to get back to the chartroom. It's still a good idea about that card file, though."

"How about the keys?"

"Right! Fink turned his set in to Mr. Morgan. But I'll lend ya mine until you get his."

Toland rested his elbow back on the chart table and studied the young man as he put the cups back down and then unhooked the flag snap holding half a dozen keys at his belt loop. He wore a small gold wedding band on the proper finger, and Toland began to admire Brock's tenacity as well as his concern for his men and his job. He recalled when he himself was a second-class quartermaster some years earlier that there had been times when he told himself there wasn't anything lower than a chief who didn't look out for his men.

"I'll take this chartroom key, and you keep the rest," Toland began, "then I'll see Mr. Morgan about the other set later. And if there's a problem, then it isn't your problem anymore, it's mine."

Brock shrugged again as he snapped his keys back on. "Maybe you think I made a mountain out of a mole hill. Well, maybe I have. And maybe I haven't. But I think if these guys don't start going ashore on liberty, and with some of their own dough in their pockets, then they might

Battlewagon

go over the hill and get some another way."
"Have you mentioned any of this to Mr. Lord?"
"His Lordship? Hell, I think Chief Gonza gives him a cut of the take. They're thick as molasses in January. Anyway, we got a tight chain of command on *Nevada,* and that's the way it should be, of course."
"And that's the way it should be, period!"
"OK, period!" Then with a smile Brock said, "Listen, Chief, this is the one that always breaks me up. Here's Sully and the Mick cleaning the bright work, or paintin' or something. Mr. Lord, he's always telling 'em to do something, but you just can't please him. 'You men there! Consider yourselves restricted!' You should hear the Mick give his imitation of Mr. Lord saying 'You men there, consider yourselves restricted!' The real joke is, they never go anywhere, anyway." The smile on Brock's face quickly faded to a shadow, as he added, "Of course, there ain't really any joke at all. When you're on a ship it's like being in prison in a way. And when you get restricted, well, it's just like somebody reminding you you're in a prison. Some of these people who hand out restrictions like they were handing out free samples ought to think about that."
"You must be some kind of shipboard philosopher around here," Toland said, half smiling. "Where's your family?"
"Seattle! Right where they ought to be."
"Any children?"
"One! A boy that looks like me."
"That's the best kind. How long you been aboard!"
"Since '38. Picked *Nevada* up in San Pedro that year. Before that I was with a makeup crew waiting to go back with the zips. But after the *Hindenburg* at Lakehurst, Washington said no more zips, so—"
"Zips?"
"Yeah! You know, Zeppelins! Dirigibles! I put over a year on the *Los Angeles*. First duty for me. After she went

35

out of commission in '32 I went aboard the *Macon* and made Third Class, and when she crashed in '35 I was home on leave, getting married. Feels like I've been on borrowed time ever since. Anyway, after those guys in Washington said no more zips I had a chance to go with the Fleet, and see what the real Navy's like. But wouldn't you know it, Mr. Morgan says he thinks they're going to quit making battlewagons one of these days and just concentrate on flattops." Brock half smiled as he shifted his weight from one leg to the other, and added, "Seems like I keep getting into things that are going out of business."

"Maybe so," Toland said, looking around the pea green-painted wheelhouse room, "but I wouldn't count these wagons out just yet."

"Don't get me wrong though, Chief. I like the Navy, and I'm goin' up for First Class next January, if I get recommended."

"Sure, we'll see," Toland said, glancing over at the Op order on the table next to him. "But first it looks like we got a busy week coming up." Then looking back at Brock, "Now what's this stuff about the Japs coming to Pearl Harbor? Plunket has a crystal ball or something?"

"It's Pollard, Chief. And what Pollard has is that old set of encyclopedias in the crew's library down on the mess decks. Every time I go down there to see him, there he is, reading away."

"Well, I guess we could all stand some mental improvement," Toland said, putting the cup to his mouth and finishing his coffee.

It began to rain, first with a whisper, then quickly growing to a noisy crescendo like the sound of a million small machine guns popping away on the weather decks and bulkheads outside.

"How come he thinks they're coming here instead of Manila or Guam or someplace like that?"

"I don't know why he thinks they're coming anywhere. I just read in this morning's paper the talks back in

Washington seem to be moving OK. It's them friggin' Nazis that worry me. Did you read where they sank the *Reuben James* day before yesterday, six hundred miles west of Iceland?"

"Yes."

"Well, anyway, Pollard keeps talking about some war the Russians and Japs had forty or fifty years ago, and a Chinese port with a funny name."

"Port Arthur, 1904."

"Yeah, that's it. Isn't that a helluva name for a Chinese port?"

"Could be," Toland answered, glancing over at the Op order again, "and could be we got a busy week coming up too."

"Right! I better check on those guys below." Brock gathered up the two empty mugs and walked to the middle ladder, then turned and made one more comment. "Pollard's a nice kid, Chief. I think he just wants to make a few friends some way. You ought to talk to him sometime, you'd like him."

"Yeah, OK, Brock. See ya!"

"Right!"

Toland refilled and lit his pipe, then turned to the Operation order in front of him and began to read in earnest those sections that would affect him and the navigation department the most. Reference was made to three specific charts, in addition to the harbor chart. They were the Local Op areas, gunfire support of Maui, and an overall Hawaiian Islands chart.

Nevada's duty bugler played a flawless Church Call over the PA system and was followed up by the bosun's command of, "Knock off all ship's work, card playing, and unnecessary talk. The smokin' lamp is out throughout the ship!"

Toland got up and stretched his legs, took one more drag from his pipe, then knocked the ashes out in the ash tray and walked over to the open hatch where he observed the tropical rain coming down on the several other gray warships around him. The waters of the harbor seemed angry at the rain for disturbing it and appeared to be attempting vainly to spit back at the gray sky.

The chief quartermaster thought briefly about Pollard's apparent theory of the Japanese forces making their attack on Pearl Harbor. That possibility had occurred to him before, but it didn't seem anymore plausible now than it did earlier. After all, Japan was some 3,500 miles over the western horizon from Honolulu. No, what she really wants is all of Southeast Asia, and the Philippine Islands come under that design. As for the events at Port Arthur almost thirty-eight years ago, it would always make interesting reading to anyone interested in Naval warfare and history, but the total comparison between Port Arthur and Pearl Harbor didn't seem logical. To begin with, Port Arthur was only about 600 miles northwest of Japan.

No, Toland thought, they would more likely come to Manila. Anyway the experts here in Honolulu and back in Washington would be hashing that one out. Then he thought Washington must be hard wanting to avoid that attack as their hands were full up with the Nazi U-boat menace that threatened the transportation of supply goods to England and Russia across the dangerous Atlantic.

The tropical rain seemed to come down even harder as Sunday wore on. It tapered off late in the afternoon, but not enough to allow the regular evening movie to be shown on the *Nevada*'s fantail. *Dawn Patrol*, starring Errol Flynn and Basil Rathbone, was shown in five reels on the crew's mess deck to an enjoying, eager audience. The rain finally died by taps.

CHAPTER III

"HEREAFTER YOU WILL CHECK THE BRIDGE URINAL TWICE A DAY!"

From an almost cloudless sky the bright Monday morning sun shone down on Pearl Harbor and her tenant vessels, warming their decks left wet by the heavy rains the day before. And from the northeast, wind streaks moved across the waters of the harbor, making it a good day for sailing.

It was 0740 when the pipe shrilled, and the bosun commanded, "Now go to your stations all the special sea and anchor detail. Go to your stations all the special sea and anchor detail! The Officer of the Deck will shift his watch from the Quarterdeck to the Bridge in five minutes. Now, muster on stations!"

Toland had had an early breakfast nearly alone in the chiefs' mess and was already on the bridge. He had brought up his mahogany box and carefully stowed it in the charthouse and was now before the chart table laying down the final track as proposed in *Nevada*'s Op order. He occasionally observed Brock and Pollard rushing around setting up the wheelhouse for getting the ship underway. Things didn't seem to be running as smoothly as they should for Brock.

The chief wanted to give his second class a chance to do his job independently, but time was running short and he knew the bridge and wheelhouse would soon be crowding up with the usual array of officers. Some would be dedicated and knowledgeable, while others often try to impress their captain at some sailor's expense who they sometimes think of in terms of being subhuman.

"Those clowns," cried Brock, "they come up here at the last minute every friggin' time. One of these days I'm going to write them both up!"

Mickey Harris was the first one swinging in from the port wing and was quickly followed by his buddy, Sullivan. "Sure sorry we're late getting up here Brock, but you shoulda seen that chow line. Hi ya, Chief!" said Mickey.

"You guys are supposed to be up here at least a half hour before sea detail," Brock answered angrily, "now, let's get with it! Pollard, you finish wiping down the windows and then get on the outside bright work. Sully, call down and get a mark on the gyro and then check out the wheel and engine-order-telegraph. Mick, you get on down to the charthouse and figure the tide and current data and come back with a set comparing watch. The 'old man's' going to want an azimuth on a bright morning like this, and, so help me God, I just want to give it to him one time when he asks for it. Now let's—"

"Something I forgot to tell you, Brock," interrupted Mickey. "Somebody stole Gazuski's camera. That dumb Polak said he came back this morning and hung it outside the head while he took his shower."

"OK, OK! Let the MAs worry about that—"

"Hey! By the way, did you guys see *Dawn Patrol* last night on the mess decks? Them fly boys, they really get the action. I shoulda been an English aviator instead of this dumb swab jockey that I am."

"Hey, Mick!" said Sullivan, "give the Chief your rendition of Basil Rathbone tellin' the guys they got to go up one more time in them Spads, to their deaths!"

"You guys are going to your deaths right now if you don't get moving. Now get moving!" demanded Brock.

"Right, Brock. Hey, Psycho! Get busy on them windows!"

After his last comment, Mickey turned and slid down

the rails of the middle ladder, making a noise through his nose like a dive-bombing airplane all the way down.

Turning to Toland, who did not appear to be amused, Brock said, with his arms up in the air, "You see what I got? Well, at least all the binoculars are in place!"

The first person other than the quartermasters to step into the wheelhouse for sea detail was the ship's navigator, Lieutenant Corbin, and was introduced to Toland by Brock. Before speaking to the chief, Corbin reminded Brock of the excess noise being made down the ladders by certain members of the navigation team.

"I hope you'll be able to do something about that, Chief."

"Yessir," answered Toland, attempting to size up the character of his new boss.

The dark, good-looking gentleman in his middle thirties needed a closer shave, and his breath was bad—he had obviously had at least one drink before coming aboard, but Toland thought his eyes had an intelligent and patient gaze about them.

"I just got the word this morning in the wardroom that you came aboard Saturday. Hope you're settled by now. Did you get a chance to look over the schedule for the week?"

"Yes," answered Toland.

Corbin moistened his lower lip, then said, "Do you have a copy with you?"

Toland produced the stapled sheets from his back pocket.

"I would like to borrow your copy for awhile, as I've seemed to misplaced my own."

The chief hesitated a moment, then handed it over. "I'll be in the charthouse for awhile. The tugs are always late anyway. Call me when they get tied up."

"Yessir," Toland answered. Then, interrupting the officer from going below, the chief brought the navigator's attention to the chart table, untaped the bottom portion of the three operational charts with their prelaid tracts, courses and rendezvous points labeled, and said, "You might want to look these over and check them against that copy."

"Yes, of course," the navigator replied, while lifting them up and studying them one by one. After a moment he hollered over his shoulder, "Brock, send down for a couple of black coffees for me and the Chief here."

The wheelhouse began to fill up with bridge personnel. Port and starboard lookouts looped binocular straps over their heads. Phone talkers were harnessing up with sound-powered phones and making contact with other talkers standing by at the bow anchor station, engine room, signal bridge, and at the forward, aft, and midship line-handling parties. Other personnel now standing by included the bosun, the messenger, and a man on the engine-order-telegraph supplied by the deck force, and the duty bugler.

The makeup of the officers included the Officer of the Deck, who would normally conn *Nevada* out to sea, taking recommendations from the navigator; the Junior Officer of the Deck, who, among his other duties, would make sure all honors were rendered and answered for involving other vessels; the Communications Officer, and Signal Officer, would run liaison from the radio room and signal bridge to the OD and captain.

"Captain's in the wheelhouse!" spoke the stern voice of the alert bosun. Everyone within earshot came to attention.

"As you were! Mr. Morgan, what is the disposition of *Tennessee* at this time?" he demanded.

"She's underway with the assistance of tugs, Captain. And *Maryland* is standing out."

"Very well! Bosun? Pass the word for the Executive Officer to report to the bridge." Then turning back to Morgan, he ordered, "Single up all lines, and have all those not actually engaged at sea detail to fall in at quarters."

"Aye, aye, Sir! Bosun, make it so!"

"Captain! The First Lieutenant desires to disconnect the phone cable at this time!" spoke the line-handling talker.

"Well, if the First Lieutenant hasn't any last-minute personal calls to make, then that's affirmative."

Everyone in the wheelhouse chuckled exactly four seconds, the time it took the captain to climb in his personal leather chair in the starboard corner of the wheelhouse, and become comfortable.

Reaching into his inside pocket, he removed the previous morning's newspaper photo featuring *Nevada*'s now-famous smokestack. Studying it at arm's length, he then called over his shoulder, "Quartermaster, some of your tape, please!"

Aware that his men were still quite busy, Toland picked up the roll he was using, walked over, and placed it in the captain's outstretched hand, then stepped back to the table.

"All lines are singled up now, Captain, and yard tugs 634 and 218 are standing by the port bow and port quarter. Do you wish lines to the tugs, sir?"

"Where's the wind, Mr. Navigator?"

Corbin, standing beside Toland, glanced nervously at the anemometer, but read it correctly as coming from, "The northeast, at eight knots, sir!"

"Then that's affirmative, Mr. Morgan," the captain replied while taping up the newspaper photo in a corner of the window directly at his right.

"Prep is too blocked, sir!" exclaimed the talker nearest Morgan.

"Very well! Bugler, sound first call to colors!"

"It appears we just might get underway on time for a change," commented the captain while getting back out of his chair and walking to the chart table. "Do you have that feeling too, Mr. Corbin?"

"It does seem possible, sir," answered the navigator as

he and Toland parted, giving the captain room to look over the proposed charts. "Saints above us, we've got a track laid down, Mr. Corbin!" the captain said in a condescending tone, "And before getting underway!" "Yes, sir!" replied Corbin. "Our first rendezvous point is with Bat Div Two at—" "I know where the first rendezvous point is, Mr. Corbin. And with whom! I am just glad you know," the captain said impatiently while looking at the bottom chart. Then looking up squarely at the officer and speaking quietly, "George, I want you to get ahold of yourself. What's done is done! Margaret is not coming back, and that's all there is to it. There's nothing more important to you than this ship—" "Captain," Corbin said, almost interrupting his commanding officer, "has the new Chief Quartermaster met you yet, Sir?" "Yes," the captain answered, turning halfway around, "Saturday afternoon, I believe. How are you, Chief!" Then turning all the way around to face Toland, "Our intrepid navigator here has had a recent bad experience, and I expect you to give him good assistance in all things pertaining to *Nevada*'s safe navigation. You do that and we'll get along." And then, pointing his finger at the chart table, added firmly, "I'm getting tired of knowing where *Nevada* 'was.' I want to know where she 'is' and where she's going!" "Execute prep!" declared the JOD in a loud voice, "Request permission to make eight bells on time, Captain!" "Permission granted, Mr. Hunt!" "Bosun, make it so! Bugler, sound colors!" The brisk rippling notes brought all topside personnel to attention and gave a chance for the officer in full commander stripes to rest a moment after he stepped into the wheelhouse. On the last note from the bugler the bosun let it be known, "The Executive Officer is on the bridge!"

"Arnold," the captain said, addressing the officer without facing him directly, "you will take *Nevada* out this morning. I think we can cast off the tugs when we come abeam of Ten-Ten-Dock. It's too nice a day, so let's shift topside and conn from the open bridge."

"Aye, aye, Captain!" answered the polished, well-built officer. He had the physical appearance of a football halfback. And as Toland later learned, he did make All-American for Annapolis in 1927 and 1928.

Stepping over to the chart table, he glanced at Toland, then quietly asked the navigator, "What's the first course off, George?"

"About 220, until we get into the center of the channel, sir."

"220, right!" Then turning to Toland, "Nice to have you with us, Chief. You have a fairly good record. However, I don't approve of those getting off and on the Navy like a seesaw, if you know what I mean."

"Yessir," answered Toland.

The XO glanced again at the top chart, then passed through the starboard hatch to join his commanding officer above the wheelhouse.

From the voice tube the captain called down in rapid-fire demand, for the barometric pressure, state of the tide, and an azimuth result. Corbin, with apparent courage to at least send up a readily available barometer reading, walked over and placed his hand on the menacing brass tube and was about to speak into it. He hesitated a moment to accept the slip of paper from Toland's hand, then read from it aloud, "Barometric pressure 30 point 18 inches and rising, the tide is on a flood at 1 knot, and we have a point 2 easterly gyro error."

"That's the way I like to hear it, Mr. Navigator. Now stand by to cast off and answer all bells, and send the steward up here with my coffee!"

"Aye, aye, sir!" answered Corbin with confidence, and relief.

At that late moment Brock reached the chief with his own hastily prepared figures. Toland accepted the slips of paper without comment, then directed his small crew to their stations; Brock at the helm, Harris on the port polaris, and Pollard on the starboard. Sullivan was already standing by his log books.

With only an occasional comment from the captain, the XO brought *Nevada* away from the mooring posts and sent her down the South Channel on the first leg out of Pearl. Both tugs were ordered off, and honors were rendered to all vessels including the *Pennsylvania* resting on blocks in Dry Dock Number One. Then keeping to the left of the dredging operations going on at the south end of the air station, *Nevada* rounded Hospital Point and steadied up on 180 until reaching Bishop Point, then made the shallow turn left to 170, the last course out of Pearl leading to the open sea.

Leaving behind the old target ship *Utah* moored on the west side of Ford Island and the drydocked *Pennsylvania* in the yard, *Nevada* departed Pearl Harbor to join the rest of her sisters for a week of intensive surface and aerial gunnery practice, with fleet maneuvers and battle formation exercises also included.

It was a beautiful day for getting underway, Toland thought to himself, as he continued recording all bearings shouted into him by Harris and Pollard. They provided the charted fixes by which the piloting courses and turns were recommended from the navigator.

It had been almost a year since he had felt a groundswell under him. And the sea breezes were like a tonic that cleared the system of old anxious thoughts and memories, both good and bad. Being at sea seemed like being home again, in a way.

But he thought *Nevada*'s navigation team could use a little polishing up. The bearings were coming in slowly and often had to be repeated. This didn't present a serious threat in broad daylight and in a familiar port, but it could under other circumstances.

"Secure the special sea detail, Mr. Hunt. And set the regular underway watch," commanded the XO upon reentering the wheelhouse, behind his captain.

"Good ship handling, Arnold. Let's go on up to seventeen knots. And I want all officers not actually on watch to report to the wardroom for briefing in fifteen minutes.

"Black smoke is reported, Sir!" declared Morgan.

"Get the Chief Engineer to the bridge!" the captain answered, with impatience.

A lieutenant commander wearing an oil-stained shirt and trousers entered the wheelhouse before the call was completed to the engine room.

"We're getting a feedback in the express tubes on number three boiler, Captain," the chief engineer declared as he saluted. "The same problem we had last week." He went into a huddle with the captain and the XO in the starboard corner of the bridge, near the taped-up newspaper clipping, to which occasional references were made.

"All right, Bruce, I hope so," declared the captain. "But I want better control than that on the weekends. Now let's get to the wardroom." On passing the chart table he added, "That means you too, George! The Chief can get us on station from here."

As *Nevada* passed Diamond Head broad on the port beam, Toland got a fresh round of bearings from his quartermasters, then recommended altering course to 135 to the new OOD, a Mr. Wheeler, who after checking his horizon did come about. From this point, and at fifteen-minute intervals, Toland laid off a series of dead-reckoned positions for the next ninety miles, more than a five-hour run. And then another forty-mile track east by northeast that would put *Nevada* on station at 1600 that evening, if all went well. After relating this navigational information to Mr. Wheeler, Toland relaxed back against the chart table wishing he had a fresh cup of coffee.

Foregoing that wish for a later moment, Toland stepped to the port wing of the bridge to join his other quartermasters. Brock had already been relieved at the wheel by the duty section helmsman.

"Hey, Chief! You didn't tell me you'd already worked out that azimuth." said Brock, his straight black hair dancing off his forehead from the stiff salt breezes.

"Yeah, Chief," put in Mickey Harris, "how come you didn't tell him! And that tide crap too."

Toland began filling his pipe as he glanced at Sullivan and then at Pollard to see if they had similar questioning faces. They did. With his pipe filled and in the corner of his mouth, he asked. "Who's got a light?"

Brock waited a long moment, then produced a book of matches.

Cupping his hands, Toland lit his tobacco then said, handing the book back to Brock, "It's everybody's beautiful day, buddy, and I sure wouldn't want to spoil yours, so I'll just let you figure that out yourself. But I'll tell you this, from now on we all get up here forty-five minutes before sea detail, and that means me, too. The first one of you that slips I'll have you back on the deck force before the sun goes down. Is that understood?"

There was no answer from the wide-eyed group, so Toland asked again, with a smile, "Understood?"

Brock remained silent as the others answered in the affirmative. Harris continued speaking, throwing a thumb in Pollard's direction, "But what about Psycho? He ain't even officially with us. He's still mess cookin'."

"Listen, Mick," Toland spoke, putting his hand on the short sailor's shoulder, "I like you, but you don't seem too bright. His name's Pollard, not Psycho! Psycho sounds like we got a bunch of nuts running around up here, and we don't want that to get around, do we! Now, I don't think he'd mind if you called him 'Encyclopedia.' Encyclopedia gives the bridge some class, like we got some brains up here. Know what I mean?"

The other quartermasters were smiling now, even Brock.

"Or better yet," continued Toland with some firmness, "you might just call him by his name, Pollard!"

"I like Encyclopedia best," answered Harris stubbornly.

"Suit yourself, buddy, but no more of that Psycho business." Then changing the subject, "Brock, take one of these men with you and round up three more sets of phones from the electricians. Bring them up here and install a set at each bearing-taker and the other at the chart table. Get the picture?"

"Gotcha. Come on, Mick!"

Toland looked at the other two men and said, "OK, Sully, better get back to your logs, and keep a fifteen-minute check going on the DR. And Pollard, you better get back down to the mess decks for now."

Alone on the port wing except for the stationary lookout some distance forward, Toland took a long drag from his pipe and observed *Maryland* and *Tennessee* in the distance with their distinct cage masts and shark bows moving off on a northwesterly course. They would round Molokai and come down on Maui's northeast side, while *Nevada*, steaming independently, would rendezvous from the south.

The brisk wind whipped around him as Toland scanned the rest of the horizon. Then, leaning back, he glanced up for a look at the vibrating signal rigging aloft. On the next deck, directly above him and within shouting distance, a chief in his late thirties smiled down at Toland. His perfect white teeth fairly glistened in his dark handsome face with a golden tan. Each guessed who the other must be. Toland knew he was smiling back at Gonza, and returned his casual salute. The chief signalman straightened his hat from its previous jaunt, then disappeared from Toland's view.

Before going back inside the chief quartermaster took three bearings; Diamond Head, right and left tangents of Oahu, then reentered the pilot house and plotted them on his chart.

"I hold you right on track, and making seventeen knots good through the water, sir!"

"Very good, Chief, thank you," answered Wheeler.

Toland looked over at Sullivan and directed him again to keep checking the DR every fifteen minutes and report any increase or decrease to the OD, and, "I'll be back up in a half hour." Then he took the middle ladder down inside *Nevada*.

Stopping by the Operations' Office, Toland met Morgan who was on his way out and carrying a blue folder under one arm. The officer gestured approval of Toland's first performance on the bridge, but indicated he was in a hurry.

"That's OK, I can pick up the keys later," Toland said.

Holding his free hand up a moment, Morgan stepped back in and said, "Shadd! Get that set of keys Fink turned in and give them to the chief here."

The Operations Yeoman left his typewriter, reached into the open safe for the keys, and tossed them to Toland.

The chief thanked both men, then each went about his own business.

The CPO mess was crowded with thirty to forty chiefs, in various coffee-drinking groups, discussing topics ranging from the crabgrass in their front lawns at home to the report of the sinking of *Reuben James* over the weekend. Finding his friend Mace at a table with Stuckey and the old gunner, referred to as Pops, Toland sat down with his steaming cup and assured them he'd had a reasonably successful sea detail his first morning underway with *Nevada*.

"Atta boy, Earl! I told you guys he could take care of himself. Now let's see what you do with God's gift to women. He's right behind ya."

Before reaching their table, Chief Gonza stopped twice to exchange kidding remarks to his other shipmates of equal grade, broke into wild laughter with a third group, and upon noticing Toland, continued smiling then took a few steps forward and sat down next to Mace, slapping him on the back. "How's the family, Charlie, old buddy? You just let me know when things ain't goin' so good between you and your old lady and I'll fix you right up. How's that, old buddy?"

Mace grimaced, more with irritation than with pain: "One of these days, Gonza, I'm goin' to deck you for sure."

"OK, OK!" laughed the chief signalman, with confidence. "And all I try to do for him is put a little love and spice in his life. Now I ask you, gents," he continued, looking around the table at Stuckey, Pops, and stopping at Toland, "is that the way to treat an old buddy?"

Toland smiled back at the powerfully built man and concluded his friend Mace would be no physical match for him, but also decided that Gonza could be largely bluff.

"Now, we're buddies, ain't we, Wheels?" said Gonza, holding out his hand.

"Sure!" answered Toland, taking his hand for a moment. Then while pulling at his ear lobe Toland said, "I got to get back up to the bridge in a minute, but I want you to do your buddy a favor."

"You just name it, buddy! You need a few bucks or something?"

"Get that kid Pollard off mess cookin' this morning. Put one of your own strikers on it. They're all standing 4 on and 12 off anyway!" Toland guessed. "You wouldn't want these QMs to be standing 4 on and 4 off if you could help it, would you?"

Gonza's eyes narrowed as his smile faded. "Why should I do that!"

"Cause we're old buddies," Toland answered, straight-faced.

A long moment passed as Stuckey leaned over to Pops

and said, "I don't think this 'buddy' thing is going to get any older."

Then Gonza broke into a beautiful grin and laughed, "We sure don't want those QMs standing 4 on and 4 off. That damn Fink, why the hell didn't he tell me? He never did talk much."

"Yeah, that's what I heard," answered Toland, sipping his coffee, then adding, "And I hear you're handling the Division great. Sure glad I ain't got it. It's always a headache."

"Yeah, always," answered Gonza, still grinning.

Toland snapped his finger, "Dammit, there's one more thing. We got to get Brock out of that compartment. He's way behind in his charts. You can handle that, can't you, buddy?" Toland now appeared amused.

Gonza's grin remained fixed, as he answered, without using the term 'buddy', "Sure! Anything else?"

Toland thought for a moment, then said, "You don't know any girls, do you?" Without giving Gonza a chance to answer, he continued. "Naw, forget it. Well, I got to get back to the bridge. See ya, Mace."

Before the noon meal *Nevada* went through man-overboard, abandon-ship, and steering-casualty drills without reducing speed or altering course. Then at 1300 GQ was sounded, as the captain, visibly irritated, demanded of the XO reasons why various departments were taking sixteen minutes to get on station and report readiness. He stated, "I'll have Zebra set in eight minutes next time, or we'll have some new Department Heads."

Toland, at the edge of his chart table, silently guessed they should be able to do it in six, and made a mental note to admonish his own quartermasters for not being on station and in battledress under 4 minutes. The day would come, he felt, when those minutes could mean the difference between life and death for some or perhaps for the entire ship.

Heavy seas began to break over *Nevada*'s ram bow, sending salt spray all the way to the bridge, and while gears and hydraulic motors down in the ship groaned, the twenty-seven-year-old machinery began moving the main battery of 14-inch gun turrets training port, then starboard. The ship stayed at GQ until 1500, giving all air and surface batteries a chance to sharpen up their handling, loading, and firing crews.

After the lookout from the crow's nest sent word down that he had spotted part of the fleet of battleships hull-down on the distant horizon, the bosun was directed to pipe an early supper for the crew.

The shutters of the 24-inch arc light above the wheelhouse banged out a 'go ahead' in answer to the flashing light from one of the distant wagons.

"BT what kept you smoky X Tom BTK."

The captain in his wheelhouse chair was having his supper from a tray. He read the message between bites, smiled, took the pencil from the messenger and scribbled, "All our newspaper friends saying aloha."

A new course of 080 was set, and at 1605 *Nevada* was on station formed up a thousand yards astern of *Tennessee*, completing the rendezvous schedule. Brightly colored bunting was sent aloft throughout the battle force, then executed, and a series of course and speed maneuvers commenced with Flagship *California* as guide.

At 1630 an 'all ships' signal from the Flag directed the Force to exercise General Quarters, and *Nevada* improved her internal readiness time down to nine minutes.

The operations officer, Lieutenant Commander Morgan, rapidly worked out tactical signals on maneuvering board problems as Corbin made his more confident recommendations to the captain after consulting the chart table.

Toland, now with his three new sets of phones fully installed and wearing one set himself, and taking visual bearings from Harris and Pollard on either wing, not only kept an accurate plot of *Nevada*'s geographical position but also that of the rest of the formation and guide as well.

Firing commenced at 1715, a little before sundown. The target plane, a PBY out of Kaneohe, pulling the black chute almost a mile behind him made eight passes up and down the formation at various levels. Three chutes plummeted into the sea as a result of good or lucky shots by *Maryland, West Virginia,* and *Oklahoma.* Screening destroyers accounted for a fourth. Bringing down a chute didn't automatically signify the only accurate firing. *Nevada*'s 5-inchers manned by fleet marines, sent up shells that exploded and put gaping holes in the long black target. Any one of which would have brought the 'enemy plane' down, if it had been an enemy plane.

The captain was more than pleased at the whole event, and before the signal went up to secure from GQ he sent his "well done" to all his antiaircraft batteries. And turning to his executive officer, said, "We'll see if the surface batteries do as good tomorrow." Then glancing over at Corbin, smiled at his navigator in recognition of his accurate recommendations. Toland returned the thumb-up signal from Morgan.

Relieved from formation, *Nevada* went up to twenty knots, heeled to port in her right turn and with Toland's own recommendation, the first the captain had directly asked of him, steadied up on 195, the best course back through Alenuihaha Channel, *Nevada*'s designated night-steam area eighteen miles southwest of the formation.

In the red glow of the dimmed wheelhouse lights, Corbin and Toland laid off ten-mile legs east and west to run against the current. And then between them agreed it had been a good day all the way around.

On Tuesday morning, the fourth of November, white caps and stiff twenty-two-knot breezes greeted the United States Pacific Battle Force engaged in continued normal peacetime exercises between the green islands of Maui and Hawaii.

Nevada's ram bow rose some thirty feet in the salt air, then came crashing down against the channel swells and lunged ahead at eighteen knots into the wind. After the helmsman steadied up, the gunnery officer, on command of the captain, exploded the twin catapult charges amidships and sent two of *Nevada*'s three scout planes aloft. The biwinged aircraft circled above at 800 feet, then came down buzzing both sides of the mother ship, and then roared off in scheduled support of the morning's firing plan. Then *Nevada* altered course and steamed northeast to rejoin the main force.

Toland expected more of a concussion than was given by his new ship's broadside firing. High in the forward conning tower, Fire Controlmen directed and recorded the hits and patterns of destruction given to Maui's southeastern coast. Explosive white charges were set off in the cliffs, simulating counterbatteries. Before she left the firing line and had moved out of range, quick gunnery readjustments were made and *Nevada* replied with two more 14-inch broadsides. The first fell short in the surf, and the other hit right on target.

As the morning wore on, the aircraft recovery detail was set, and *Nevada* maneuvered to retrieve her two bobbing float planes from the heavy seas.

After the noon meal *Nevada* went to GQ once more and laid down another barrage on the island and then secured from the day's heavy gunnery practice.

The gunnery officer was reached by phone and directed to come to the bridge at the captain's request. Lieutenant Finch was pleased at his captain's favorable remarks but indicated a desire to get in more antiaircraft firing practice.

"Nonsense, Mr. Finch, you're doing fine. Anyway, we've got to keep to schedule." Then, turning to Corbin, "George, give us a course and speed to arrive back at our night-steam area by sunset."

Toland was ready for it, and with pencil in hand added a few more numbers, then drew a circle around the figures '198, 14 kts' in the lower right-hand corner of the chart.

Corbin, observing Toland's actions, picked up the dividers and measured off the distance from the chief's last DR. He glanced at the deck clock, then repeated aloud the circled figures to the captain while smiling at Toland.

"That's the way I like to hear it, George," said the captain, nodding to the OD to follow the navigator's recommendations, then, "Bosun! Set the regular underway watch and pass the word for all officers not actually on watch to lay to the wardroom for critique."

Hauling thirty degrees to starboard the battleship answered the helmsman's wheel motions, and Toland bent over the chart to lay down the new track.

Brock, after having been relieved at the wheel, walked over and leaned close to his chief, and in a quiet voice let Toland know that Pollard had been let off from mess cooking and would be taking the first watch with him. While intently observing the chief quartermaster's precise handling of the protractor and compass dividers, he added, "The captain, he don't holler at Mr. Corbin so much anymore."

"And Mr. Corbin doesn't holler at me, and I don't holler at you," Toland said without looking up from his work. "And that's because you and the other guys have been doing a good job." The chief then looked straight at Brock. He meant it.

"Now go out and get me a cut on Kauiki Head, Puhilele Point, and Nuu Landing."

Brock hustled to the starboard wing, moved the bearing circle around to the three selected points on Maui's southern coast, then returned to the chart table with the figures. While plotting the fresh fix, Toland asked, "How's the weather, buddy?"

"The wind has died down, and we got about a number '2' sea state."

"OK, Brock," he said, handing him the pencil, "we're right on track. Keep your fixes going every fifteen minutes. And keep the OD informed.

"Right, Chief!"

Toland smiled at his number one assistant, then departed the bridge.

Halfway down the ladder he heard, then saw, his friend, Charlie Mace who was in a heated argument with Ensign Lord just outside the radio room.

"Hereafter, Mace, you will check the bridge urinal twice a day yourself, and then there will be no need to order you around in front of your men!"

"There never has been and there ain't never gonna be a need for you to order me around in front of my men. I got a man policing that damn bridge urinal once in the morning and once in the afternoon. I can't help it if some officer decides to puke in there right after it was cleaned up. I can't check on it every—"

"Are you disobeying my orders?"

"Maybe it was you that puked in it."

"Direct disobedience of orders and insubordination. You wouldn't be so damn smart if I had a witness!" the young ensign declared, and then he happily noticed Toland, who was backing up from the bottom of the ladder.

"Toland! Chief Toland! I need you here. Right now."

"You son of a—" Mace muttered without finishing.

"Did you hear that, Toland?"

"I haven't heard anything here, Mr. Lord," Toland answered. "But I've heard Chief Mace is a good radioman and does his job, and his men respect him. At least that's what I've heard, sir."

The ensign's lips tightened up and turned inward for a moment. Then he said, "Neither one of you have heard the end of this yet. You'll see!" Then he left by way of the wardroom ladder. About halfway down to the next deck the angry officer lost his footing because of a sudden upward movement made by *Nevada* rolling in the heavy swells. Mace started down to give him a hand, but Ensign Lord shrugged it off in continued anger.

CHAPTER IV

"WE WEREN'T READY.
WE JUST WEREN'T READY FOR 'EM."

Motioning his heated friend out through the port hatch, and into the fresh early evening breezes, Toland noticed for the first time how much Mace had aged and this meant, of course, he had aged, too.

"Still pulling me out of jams, buddy?" said Mace, taking a deep breath and leaning on the sponson deck rail.

"No, and you're not in any jam. But you could be later if you're not careful. And we ain't kids anymore either. Anyway, our young Mr. Lord may be a pretty unhappy man right now."

"That's another thing that's getting me, Earl. We put sixteen years in this lashup, and a whole lot of ships behind us, then along comes a squirt like that and the Navy tells him to fill out my quarterly marks. He'll be filling yours out too, buddy, come next January. Hell, he ain't much older than sixteen right now. And this is his first ship. Just how do you figure that!"

"Well," Toland smiled, "the Navy says he's smarter than you and me."

"Smarter! Dammit, I've got twelve radiomen in there, over a dozen typewriters and code keys to keep moving, two thousand channels and circuits and a half dozen frequencies to guard night and day, and that squirt couldn't park a three-wheeled bike and you know it. The least the Navy could do is see to it that those who are designated to fill out our quarterly marks could at least park a two-wheeled bike. What do you say, Earl?"

The PA system clicked open throughout the ship, and the duty bosun passed the word, "Now, the evening movie to be shown on the fantail at 2000 will be *Mutiny on the Bounty* with Clark Gable and Charles Laughton. Also, Talent Night from 17 to 1900. Those wishing to participate, see Ensign Toby in the ship's office."

The two chiefs looked at each other and smiled, and Toland said, "I say let's get down and shower before those other guys get all the hot water, then grab some quick chow and take in the flick."

"Hey listen, buddy," Mace said over his shoulder to Toland, who was hurriedly following him down the second deck weather ladder, "don't leave out our Talent Night. *Nevada*'s got some pretty good characters on her, you just wait and see."

Seated at the supper table after having cleaned up, Mace continued speaking highly of *Nevada*'s weekly Talent Night. "And we got these three guys from the stewards' pantry. They do a takeoff on the Ink Spots that—"

"Sorry to interrupt you, Chief," one of the CPO mess cooks broke in, "but the radio shack called and said to tell you they got a coded group message to break and want you up there."

Without speaking in return, Mace took two more quick bites and got up from the table while downing half his coffee, then said, on reaching for his hat, "Save me a chair on the fantail, Earl."

Toland nodded in affirmative and went back to finishing his dinner.

"Movies, floor shows. What's this Navy coming to? Next thing you know we'll be having women in the Navy."

"That wouldn't be such a bad idea, Pops," Mace said good-naturedly, "but you'd be sore because you couldn't handle any of 'em!" then unfairly departed without giving the old gunner a chance to reply.

Smiling sympathetically at the aging chief, Toland got

up for another cup of coffee, then accepted an invitation to join him and his gunner's mate friend of near age at the far end of the mess table.

"Lacey! This is that Quartermaster that upset Gonza's applecart," he said in his gravel voice.

"I don't think I've upset anybody yet," Toland said with a smile, while shaking hands.

"What's holding you back, son?" answered Lacey.

"Well, I haven't seen his girlfriends yet."

All three men laughed simultaneously. The conversation stayed on the subject of women as Pops began with, "I nearly got married once myself—you didn't know that did you, Lacey! It was that last night in 'Frisco back in '23 before we ran aground."

"You never mentioned that part before," answered Lacey, indicating he had heard his story of the grounding a few times but not this new additional sequence.

"Well that's because I've been keeping it private, until now. She was from Liverpool."

"Liverpool?" asked Lacey, accepting dessert from one of the mess cooks.

"That's what I said, wasn't it? Liverpool! She'd only come to our country a few months before. And she was working at the greeting card counter in the Emporium there on Market Street." Lacey looked disbelieving, and the older gunner added firmly, "It was my dear father's birthday coming up, September 12th, and I was buying him a card."

"Well, get on with it. What happened!" interrupted Lacey while taking another bite of his apple pie.

"Well, it was right after President Harding died in the old Palace Hotel in 'Frisco, and we had just been escortin' him around Alaska and Puget Sound the month before. Just goes to show, you never know. Well anyway, we steamed back to 'Frisco for Fleet Week and nested at Pier 15 just up from the old Ferry Building, until that last night. I was sure glad I had the liberty 'cause I wanted to get that card for my dear father. And that's when I met Maude."

"Maude?" Lacey asked, doubtfully.

"Maude! That's what I said, wasn't it? Say, are you getting hard of hearing, Lacey? Anyway, Wheels, we made a date and I waited until she got off work, then we went to Chinatown for dinner. Then we took the cable car over to her place at," he looked up in the air thoughtfully, then said, "Sacramento and Walnut. And the next morning we got underway for San Diego, only we ran aground on the Honda Reef before—"

"Wait a minute. What do you mean, the next morning you got underway. What happened at Sacramento and Walnut?" demanded Lacey.

Pops looked genuinely irritated at being interrupted by his friend again, but patiently decided to complete the story. "Well, Maude was a real fine woman. The kind that considered love and marriage inseparable. We argued over it until three in the morning. She won the argument all right, and I agreed at three-thirty that since we were both so deeply in love that marriage should be entered into, along with any other activities we might wish to pursue. She saw me to the cable car at half-past six."

"Damn you, gunner! You never told me that part before. I don't believe it anyway!"

"I didn't tell you, because it was private!"

Toland smiled then asked, "What ship in line were you!"

"The *Young*! Right behind *Lee* and *Delphy*, and followed by *Woodbury, Nichols*, and *Farragut*. Only *Farragut* steered clear, but coming on fast was *Fuller* and *Chauncey*. Out there hanging onto the *Young*'s side that cold, wet morning I always wondered if maybe Maude didn't wish some of her London fog down on us."

"I thought you said she was from Liverpool!" said Lacey, in a loud voice.

"That's right, Liverpool! But London's not far from Liverpool, and London probably gets a lot more fog. Anyway, Wheels, old Cal Coolidge really hit the overhead on that one. It's a good thing Cal wasn't the president when the Japs bombed Lacey and the *Panay*. He'd 'a declared war on 'em the next day."

"Bilge water!" said Lacey, pushing his empty plate away. "Keep cool with Coolidge. I heard someone had to light a fire under him every morning at the White House just to get him out of bed."

It looked to Toland they might be getting into a political argument so he steered the conversation directly to the *Panay*, as he remembered seeing the small gunboat once or twice tied up to Poo Tung Wharf across from Shanghai some years earlier anyway.

"Hell, yes," answered Lacey. "We tied up there lots of times. Two or three months at a stretch sometimes. What ship did you say you were on then?"

"*Fox*!"

"Hell, yes, the *Fox* 234, old four piper. Used to moor up to the midchannel buoys on the old Wang Poo, down from Queen's Jetty Landing. Hey, where did you pull your liberties! Paramount? Chung Hee's? Ding How's? Mama Sue's! I got thrown out of all them joints at one time or another."

"We can believe that!" said the old gunner.

"Dee Dee's?" mentioned Toland, taking a sip of his coffee.

"Oh yeah," returned Lacey, in long low tones, "in the French Quarter on—, on—"

"Avenue Fosh!" said Toland.

"Yeah, Avenue Fosh, near Bubbling Well Road. But that really wasn't a joint. Just a nice place to eat. I remember they had a good lookin' dame playin' piano there. But I tell ya, the best place in town to go was the old Fifth Marine Barracks off Nanking Road, right downtown where the action was. I got my initials carved on one of them mahogany tables in there just like everybody else. I bet every Jar Head or Swabby that ever passed through

Shanghai carved his initials on one of them tables."

"How long were you on the *Panay*?" asked Toland.

"From the cradle to the grave," answered Lacey. "I was a plank owner. Put her in commission right there in Shanghai where she was built. Kiangnan Dock, November 11, 1927. A hundred and ninety-one feet long and a twenty-eight-foot beam. She wasn't much for looks, but she could get up and go, up to eighteen knots along that Yangtze when she wanted to. Had to sometimes, just to get out of the way of them junks. They wouldn't get out of the way if the devil himself were bearing down on 'em."

"But that wasn't fast enough for those Jap planes, was it, Lacey?" asked the gunner sympathetically.

"No, it wasn't. We were anchored anyway," he admitted, "about twenty miles up from Nanking. The Japs were movin' in to take Nanking, and we moved up to that little cove, with three oilers, to get out of the way of shore fire. And here those two bastards came, out of the sun. They couldn't possibly have missed seeing the American flags we had painted on the top decks. The thing that will always get me, though, is that we weren't ready. We just weren't ready for 'em. We had two 3-inch 50s and never got one of them off. The rifle and small-arms fire we sent up didn't do much good, except make us feel a little better about it. Anyway, she went to the bottom of the Yangtze the twelfth of December, 1937.

"What day was it?"

"Sunday!"

Two bells sounded over the PA system. Toland finished his coffee and pushed himself up from the table.

Charlie Mace was right, Toland thought, as he found a couple of seats in the CPO viewing section. The sun was just going down off the starboard quarter as the three Negro musicians began delivering their first song to a cheering crew on *Nevada*'s fantail. "I Don't Want to Set the World on Fire" was an expert carbon of the Ink Spots.

64

Their next song, with a little act thrown in, tickled everyone—"Jim Doesn't Ever Bring Me Pretty Flowers."

"Hey, Earl, what'd I tell ya? Ain't they good?" came Mace's voice as he slid in and occupied the empty seat at Toland's left. "But I got bad news. Corbin sent word down he wants you to give a celestial navigation lecture to some junior officers that are waiting on the bridge, right now."

Visibly irritated, Toland nevertheless looked up and scanned the cloudless deepening blue sky and spotted what he felt was probably Vega just beginning to twinkle high in the northeastern quadrant.

While in plain sight of land there was no necessity for shooting evening stars to locate *Nevada*'s position, but the celestial conditions did lend themselves to good sextant practice. He would have to hurry if he was going to do any shooting at all, as there would be a million stars out in a half hour, and it would be difficult to tell one from the other through the sextant scope.

Toland rose from his seat, promising Mace he would return if he finished early enough, then made his way through the cheering crowd on the fantail, continued on forward, and climbed up to the charthouse.

The chief quartermaster quickly worked out a local-hour-angle from *Nevada*'s dead-reckoned position and the *Nautical Almanac*. He figured an estimated azimuth and declination for four selected stars; Fomalhaut, Vega, Alphy, and Deneb. He then got his jacket on, put a flashlight and a couple of pencils in his left pocket, and a set stopwatch and the sight log in the other. Then, for the first time in over a year, he carefully removed his British-made Husun sextant from its mahogany box. He had been carrying it around all over the China Sea and Pacific Ocean for the better part of the 1930s.

On the open bridge above the wheelhouse Chief Toland courteously approached the three young junior officers, each already in possession of a standard Navy Bendix sextant, and proceeded to instruct them in its proper usage. Then with professional precision he located the four selected stars, now twinkling brightly, and brought each in succession down smartly to the clear horizon, calling, "Stand by,-mark!"

While the eager young officers sighted and recorded for each other, Toland found it difficult to push from his mind the recent interesting conversation with his two shipmate chiefs, especially the remarks concerning the *Panay*. It was the first he had heard she was actually at anchor at the time of the attack.

An ill feeling of sorts began to set with him as he gazed at the last faint rays of sunset in the darkening western sky. *Nevada*'s running lights shone brightly, and the up-and-down laughter and cheers swelling up from the thoroughly amused sailors on the fantail only seemed to deepen his apprehension.

"OK, Chief, we got 'em! What's next?"

"Well, sir," Toland began, giving his full attention back to his future 'admirals,' "next we head for the charthouse and four hot coffees."

To Toland's surprise, the young men did better than he expected. After twenty-five minutes of consulting the *Nautical Almanac* again and extracting the proper figures from HO 214, volume three, he applied that information to a standard navigational form. Then with dividers and parallel rulers, the chief quartermaster carefully plotted the assembled results to the correct plotting sheet.

His own celestial fix had a triangle of less than a quarter mile, while his 'students' presented fixes of less than two miles each. All were within three miles of *Nevada*'s DR. A 'tare victor george' in any navigators' book. But these were calm seas, good horizons, and it was a clear night. He cautioned, "The elements are not always so obliging." The young navigators nevertheless remained undaunted.

Although *Nevada*'s schedule called for a full week of operations, she would put only one more day, and night at sea for continued training. It would be her last until the first week of December.

On the morning of the fourth day out, and while *Nevada* again raced northeast to rejoin the Battle Force for another day of exercises, Toland spotted Corbin alone on the port wing of the bridge observing the seas and apparently enjoying the brisk weather.

Taking advantage of his opportunity to speak with him alone, Toland pulled up his jacket collar and approached the officer. After the two men exchanged greetings, he proceeded to inform the navigator as to the slack condition the charts and publications had reached, and offered him the same possible solutions he had spoken of with Brock on the previous Sunday.

Corbin listened to his assistant navigator with interest and with what appeared to be respect. Then he nodded and said, "That seems to be the best way to handle it all right. Probably should have approached it from that quarter long before now." Then, with a smile, "We'll see how it works out. Thank you for bringing it to my attention."

With the conversation over, Toland saluted again and reentered the wheelhouse. Passing the navigation table on his way to the chartroom below, he leaned over and directed Brock to send down one of the quartermasters.

"Right!" Brock answered, then said, "Hey, Chief, I ain't got the Compartment PO anymore."

Toland paused a moment, then leaned back over the table. "That's good buddy, now you got more time to get those charts and pubs in order. But first," said Toland, looking over Brock's shoulder, "what the hell we got going on over there?"

Earlier, the second-class quartermaster had ordered his men up in full force to 'field day' the wheelhouse, taking advantage of the lull in activity to get the bridge shipshape. He had Pollard on the windows, Sullivan on the .

bright work, and Mickey Harris swabbing down the deck. But now, as he looked back over his shoulder, what he saw was Pollard grinning down from his window work, and Sullivan doubled up in an effort to keep from laughing out loud at his friend, Mickey, sitting up in the captain's chair emulating his commanding officer's pained expressions over the newspaper clipping still taped to the side window.

Even the man at the wheel enjoyed the show.

"Mind your rudder, Helmsman!" demanded the officer of the deck, without taking his eyes from his binoculars as he scanned the horizon for remnants of the Battle Force.

Mickey turned around in the captain's chair and soundlessly began to mouth the OD's words in authoritative fashion. He then saw Brock and Toland firmly staring back at him, at which he leaped from the leather chair to the deck, quickly retrieved the wet mop from against the binnacle, and began a vigorous swabbing of the wheelhouse deck.

The OD shifted his gaze from the horizon to the small commotion behind him only in time to see a dedicated American sailor doing a good job at turning-to.

"That bastard!" Brock muttered, straining to keep his own voice down. "He saw that movie last night, and now he thinks he's Mr. Christian or something." Then Brock shook his head and smiled in despair.

His smile quickly faded as he glanced at his chief quartermaster, who, instead of smiling in return, said, "You get that friggin' sailor squared away!"

"Right, Chief!" was Brock's answer, as Toland turned and left the bridge.

Alone inside the charthouse Toland now felt free to chuckle a moment at Mickey's comedy. Then after setting himself on one of the high stools before the chronometer case, he poured himself a half cup of very black coffee.

Spinning around on the stool, Toland scanned the shelves of jammed-in books, pamphlets, and periodicals. As he contemplated shifting some of the navigational material that was of no immediate use, to the storeroom, his eyes stopped at an unrelated publication shoved back between Volume 9 of HO 214, and *Polar Navigation.* It was a hardback copy of *The World Almanac 1941*, published by the *New York Sun.*

Toland began thumbing through from the middle of the thick book and finally stopped at the inside cover. There a neat hand had penned, "To Jimmy. Smooth sailing in the U.S. Navy. Your friend, Paula."

The charthouse door swung open with the sway of the ship, and Pollard stepped in wearing a grin that faded on noticing the book in the chief's hands.

"Brock sent me down."

Looking at Pollard, then the book, and back at Pollard again, "You Jimmy?"

"Yes, sir."

"Well, this is a good book to have, Jimmy. Maybe we need one of these up here. But the fact is," Toland said, handing the book to the young sailor and looking around the room, "we got a lot of charts and publications up here we don't really need, and I want one of you to stow about half of it in the navigation storeroom when we return to port."

As Pollard listened attentively, Toland called off a number of volumes and portfolios that fell in the unneeded category.

"Well, that's enough to give us a little breathing room for a while. What do you say?"

"Four oh, Chief!"

Toland smiled at the young man's effort at sounding salty, then asked him to help himself to some coffee.

"What made you get in the Navy, Jimmy?"

"It was my dad!" he answered, trying to conceal his distaste for black, sugarless coffee. "He was on the *Rhode Island,* and then on the *Michigan.* He saw lots of action in the Navy during the Great War."

Toland sipped his coffee and listened to the young man a

while. Then he interrupted Pollard because of a gross error in Naval history the young man had just made concerning his father's exploits, but too late in deciding it may have been his father's error and not his son's exaggeration.

"There were no American ships in the Battle of Jutland, Pollard. The nearest one was—" But it was too late. "Well, I don't think there was."

While Pollard put his cup back in the rack, Toland clinched his jaw at his own error, then guessed it may have been many months since this young man had talked to an interested adult. And he admitted to himself he was interested in some of Pollard's notions.

"Sit back down, Jimmy. I'd like to hear why you think the Japs are coming to Pearl Harbor. That is what you said, isn't it? The Japanese are coming to Pearl Harbor?"

"Yes! I said it." Pollard shrugged his thin shoulders, adding, "But I don't know it. Just guessing." Then he said, looking up at the overhead, "I'd sure like to be friends with all the guys."

"And you think," said Toland softly, "that by seeming to be as smart or a little smarter than they are they'll like you for it?"

Pollard's face turned a little red with embarrassment, but didn't answer.

"Well, I got a bulletin for you, buddy. They just might hate you for it. Not intentionally, of course, but they just might. You understand, Jimmy?"

Pollard hesitated a moment, then said, "Yes sir, I think so."

"And I'm not a 'Sir.' " Toland said with a half smile. "Now, I'd like to hear why you think the Japs are coming to Pearl. I think they're going to hit Manila myself."

"Well," he began, "because the Navy's in Pearl."

"We got a Navy in Caviti, too."

"As big as what's in Pearl Harbor?" asked Pollard.

"Maybe not, but the British and Dutch have a lot of sea power in that area too, and the Philippines are a damn

70

sight closer to French Indochina and Tokyo than Pearl.

"Look, Chief," Pollard said, turning the pages of his girlfriend's gift, and stopping at 'Marine Disasters'— "Look here!"

As Toland took the book from Pollard's hand, he felt a reduction of *Nevada*'s speed, but began reading anyway, the paragraph the young sailor pointed to.

"Russo-Japanese War, 1904-05. Began with surprise attack on Russian Fleet at Port Arthur, Feb. 9, 1904. Battle of Tsushima Bay. May 27, 1905. Japanese Fleet under Adm. H. Togo, destroyed Russian Fleet under Adm. Z. Rojdestvensky. Russian losses, 5 battleships, 5 cruisers, and 10,000 men. Japanese losses, 3 torpedo boats and casualties under 1,000 men."

Handing the book back to Pollard, Toland thoughtfully commented, "She's been after full control of that part of the world for a long time all right, but Pearl is a long way from there. And Port Arthur and Tsushima are right in her own back yard."

"Yes, but ships can travel a lot farther now than they used to in those days, can't they, Chief?" Pollard asked shyly, "Maybe she thinks our fleet is the only thing that's standing in the way of what she wants."

"Maybe so," Toland answered thoughtfully. He was about to add that he hoped the Japanese would have better sense than attack the United States anywhere, but the chartroom door opened abruptly with Sullivan putting his head in.

"Hey, Chief, the port engine is going off the line, and we're heading in. Going to tie up to the piers, maybe Ten-Ten Dock. I'll bet we'll be laid up for a month."

It must have been true, Toland thought, as he felt *Nevada* begin heeling to port in a sharp turnabout.

"OK, Sully, you go back up and start laying down the charts for going in. I'll be up in a minute. Pollard! Don't forget to shift those charts and pubs below after we secure."

"Something else, too, Chief," Sully remarked. "They

caught the guy that swiped Gazuski's camera. Gonza and the MA's got him on the mess decks right now. It was that feather-merchant, Shadd."

On the bridge Toland found a full array of ships' control officers, including the captain, who was speaking to the chief engineer.

"All right, Bruce, these things happen. The Port Director says Ten-Ten Dock is empty, so we'll be right next to the shipyard. Meanwhile, can you continue to give us full power on the starboard unit?"

"Aye, Captain! She's sound as a dollar there. And I should be able to give you about 10 percent from the port fireroom in thirty minutes."

"Captain!" the communications officer broke in, "Message received from the Flag, 'You are relieved from scheduled exercises. Proceed Pearl independently.' "

The commanding officer then turned to the chart table, and, in Corbin's absence from the bridge, "Chief, give me a course and ETA to the sea buoy at—twelve knots," and over his shoulder, "twelve about right, Bruce?"

"Twelve knots is good, sir!"

From his newly plotted fix, Toland was able to quickly recommend holding 270 for 55 minutes, round Smuggler Cove at 0940, then a direct course in on 305, arriving at the first sea buoy at 1710. Having accepted his chief quartermaster's recommendations, the captain then drafted a radio message back to the Port Director at Pearl Harbor requesting tug assistance on arrival at 1730.

Toland remained on the bridge with Brock until *Nevada* rounded Smuggler Cove at the southwest end of Kahoolawe Island, then went below.

Scuttlebut passed quickly and the chiefs' mess was alive with Navy men anxious to get back in port again. For many it meant being home with their families sooner than they had expected.

"Well, buddy, just about forty more shopping days till

Christmas. You gonna get your kids something, aren't you?"

"I'll get 'em something," answered Toland.

"You wanta go shopping with me and Doris? We're gonna beat the Christmas rush! But we ain't going until next week though." Mace took another sip of his coffee and said, "Monday's pay call. You wanta go out with us next week?"

"I don't know. I'll let you know next week."

"Listen, you got to do your shopping early so's you can mail it off and get it Stateside by Christmas." Then he smiled, "Come on, Earl, what you gonna get your kids for Christmas?"

Toland was somewhat irritated and he was about to give his friend a sharp reply, but realized in time that Mace was only trying to be helpful and meant well.

"I don't know yet, buddy, just haven't given it much thought, I guess."

"Well, it's about time you do. Christmas don't wait for nobody, ya know. Hey, Doris is gonna be real surprised to see me bring you home tonight."

Toland began observing Gonza at the next table over, commenting on his expert handling of Shadd after catching him in the act of hiding the missing camera in his overnight bag.

"Hey Earl, you got liberty weekend don't you?"

"Yeah, I think so."

"You think so! You got to know them things, buddy. What section did you get assigned to?"

"Five, I think."

"Let's see," said Mace, pulling out his wallet and removing a card calendar with several markings on it. "You won't have a duty weekend until the 29th and 30th of this month. I'm free until the 6th and 7th of December. Hey, are you listening to me!"

"Yeah, I'm listening. I was just wondering what makes a Third-Class Yeoman swipe a three dollar camera.

Gonza just said it was a three-dollar Brownie."

"Yeah, that's what it was all right. I saw it, and Morgan told me I got to supply an Operations Yeoman till after Shadd's mast. Gonza, that loudmouth bastard. He coulda handled Shadd and that camera thing a lot better than what he did. And he keeps going around tellin' everybody how he hates a thief. I'll tell you what he hates. After checking his books he found Shadd owed thirty-five dollars to his slush fund. You ought to take over the Division Earl, and you know it."

"I'll tell you what I ought to do, buddy," Toland said, finishing off his coffee and rising from the table, "go back up and work on the noon posit for the twelve o'clock reports. That's what I ought to do!"

By midafternoon the seas were relatively calm, and orders went out from the XO to get the ship cleaned up before entering port. Gunner's mates and their strikers were put busy cleaning *Nevada*'s enormous gun barrels and turrets, while seamen washed down the caked salt from her weather bulkheads, then holy-stoned her teakwood decks to a smooth white finish.

Through a slight haze, landfall on Oahu was made at 1625. Shortly after passing Diamond Head starboard abeam, the mouth of the naval harbor came into full view. On the bridge, the captain ordered his OD to reduce *Nevada*'s speed even more, allowing a wide distance between his ship and the Carrier Task Force standing out to sea from Pearl.

Forming up on a westerly course, *Enterprise*, flanked by three swayback cruisers and nine screening destroyers, headed off into the proverbial sunset.

There was no doubt as to the identity of the big aircraft carrier, her silhouette being decidedly different from the other three American flattops in the Pacific. The old *Langley*, the first U.S. carrier, on duty in Philippine waters. *Saratoga*, in for repairs at San Diego. Leaving only *Lexington* and *Enterprise*, operating out of Pearl Harbor.

Whistle signals and searchlights adequately pene-
trated the early evening darkness as the first lines went
over from *Nevada*'s bow and down to the swarm of shipyard workers along the sea wall, while two gray Navy tugs
nuzzled their cumbersome burden snug against Ten-
Ten-Dock.

CHAPTER V

"YOU LIKEY MI LING?–
"HAVE YOU EVER BEEN SUNK AT
PORT ARTHUR?"

The battered taxicab rumbled along the unpaved highway a while longer, jostling the driver and his four passengers up and down, this way and that. Then they abruptly settled to a smoother ride as the dusty black Ford left the gravel road leaving Pearl Harbor Naval Base behind and continued on the asphalt road going in to Honolulu.

The cabby interrupted his own train of conversation to make a comment about how the city should finish paving the road, then went back to what he had previously been saying. "Anyway, them Japs know we mean business this time. They ain't gonna do anything else. It's them Nazis we gotta worry about. You guys are real lucky you're here instead of in the Atlantic."

"Yeah, we're real lucky," answered the sailor in the front seat next to the cabby. "You got a radio in this buggy?"

"Well, you are lucky! I got a letter from my wife's brother who works in a shipyard in Boston, and he says them U-boats are sinking everything in sight. And no, I haven't got a radio in this buggy. You don't see one, do ya?"

"Say, now there's something we can all feel lucky about."

"What's that!"

"You and your brother-in-law are on our side."

76

The cab driver cast a stern look at the passenger to his right who had just cocked his white hat on the brim on his nose.

"Knock it off, Boyle" directed the sailor sitting in the middle of the rear seat. "He didn't mean anything by it, mister. Anyway, Boyle's already got a brother in the Atlantic right now."

This seemed to satisfy the driver, and he too admitted that he meant no offense. Then he continued on with his opinions of the world situation, remarking at one point that he was too young to serve in the last war and feared he was too old for the one coming up.

Toland, sitting in the corner next to the left window, paid little attention to the conversation and instead observed the few small changes that had taken place along King Street since his last duty in the Pacific. This section of the city had always reminded him of New Orleans with its iron and grill work over the balconies. Now, a few more houses had gone up west of the city, there were more telephone poles, and the road had been paved a little closer to Pearl Harbor than before.

On the previous evening, after *Nevada* finally tied up portside to, Toland secured from sea detail, met with Mace in the chiefs' quarters, and declined his offer of meeting his family that night. He was tired and wanted to stay on board. His friend hurried with his shower and shave, and Toland promised he would call him at his home sometime the next day. Still in a hurry, Mace had reached in the back of his locker and pulled out a bright multicolored silk sport shirt and tossed it to the chief quartermaster, saying, "You're out of uniform in town without one of these things on, buddy."

When Mace was fully dressed and ready to leave the ship, he scribbled down his home address, and a number for Toland to call when he was in town, explaining it was a next door neighbor's phone. They were nice people and didn't mind him using it.

Before turning in, Toland dug through his own gear and pulled out two crumpled sets of whites and gave them to the duty mess cook to be laundered and pressed by the next day.

And now it was the next day, Friday, November 7. Early liberty had been granted for all hands except the duty section and those actually engaged in engine-room activities. In the chiefs' mess, Gonza tried but met with no success in his efforts to gain a standby for his scheduled Friday duty. So instead he got up a five-handed poker game for the evening with a few other chiefs who had the duty.

Two gangways had been set in place, the one aft for the officers and the forward gangway for enlisted personnel. Stores and machinery parts would be loaded or unloaded night and day. At 1410, Toland saluted the Quarterdeck with Chief Darnell in charge, then crossed over the forward gangway in fresh starched whites, and holding a brown paper bag under his arm.

Chipping hammers, moving cranes, riveting and welding instruments created an ear-piercing racket around him as Toland walked through the shipyard filled with cruisers and destroyers and packed in the familiar Baker Docks for repairs and overhauls. A slow-moving vehicle, affectionately known in the area as a 'leaping tuna,' overtook the chief, moving a little faster than he could walk, so he casually stepped on board and joined several other sailors, mostly in dungarees, on its hourly voyage around the Yard.

He jumped off as it neared the Main Gate. Then, realizing he had just missed the last bus, joined three other sailors paying twenty-five cents each, in advance, for a taxi ride into town. And now giving only slight attention to the talkative cab driver, Toland shifted in his corner to watch several children at play in Aala Park going by; then the scene passed completely from his view.

The taxi continued on through the Chinese quarter, and

through the open-air market districts. The sky darkened, and a few merchants appeared to be shifting umbrellas over their goods to protect them from the approaching afternoon shower.

On passing Iolani Palace to his left, Toland called to the driver to pull up.

"I'm going all the way to Thomas Square, Chief."

"No, this is OK."

As he stood a few feet off the curb waiting for the traffic to pass, the clock set high in the steeple above the columns of the ancient old Kawaiiahao Church behind him read five after three.

A few large rain drops struck the brim of his hat and shoulders as he gripped the paper sack and darted through an opening in the traffic, crossed the intersection of Punchbowl and King streets, and mounted the steps of the Honolulu Public Library on the other side.

He hadn't originally intended to spend the afternoon among a lot of books, but it was too early to visit with his old friend Cho Han back in Chinatown, even if he was still there. Anyway, the events of Port Arthur gnawed at him, and Pollard's suggestion that the Japanese Fleet now had greater mobility and range further intrigued him.

The Battle of Tsushima posed no real history lesson to Toland. He was well informed of those naval actions on the high seas off the southern coast of Korea, and their results. Port Arthur, on the other hand, seemed one of those nasty affairs that shouldn't have taken place and one unbefitting the brilliant Admiral Togo.

But it was precisely this kind of Japanese military action over the years; undeclared wars, surprise attacks, humbling and humiliating her enemies into an early suit for peace, and winning for her more and more territory, that made Toland feel she would attack again, and soon. It was not Port Arthur but a collection of 'Port Arthurs' that brought him to his conclusion. He had not studied any of them in depth; he only knew that they had happened. And she always seemed to attack in or near the area she wanted. Consequently, Manila seemed the most logical target.

And now with Pollard's notions on the subject, regardless of whether they were sincere or just a matter of being different simply for the sake of winning some new friends, it was enough to interest Toland into a deeper study of all the 'Port Arthurs.'

True, Toland was only an enlisted man. His conclusions wouldn't alter any course in history. But he would be ready to meet history if and when it came and to be a part of it in the best way he could, and perhaps guide his own men into making a better account of themselves than they might otherwise do on their own. But he was still determined to leave the Navy when his present enlistment was up. All this 'sir' business to nearly teenagers who had hardly begun to shave yet was beginning to get on his nerves.

Without pausing to ask questions, Toland walked past the main desk and wandered through the first floor of the library. The north end was mostly for childrens' reading, where several giggling youngsters were being asked to quiet down by one of the pert librarians of Oriental descent.

At the south end Toland found the section he was looking for—World History and Political affairs. Placing his hat and brown paper bag on one of the empty reference tables, he turned to face the mountain of volumes neatly stacked along the inboard case.

After eight to ten minutes of scanning titles and authors, he sat down with three selections. The first contained a modern history of Japan; the second was on China. The third was a heavy work on the last world war, of which he began reading first, skipping over the unrelated parts.

The rain outside continued to shower for some time. It stopped abruptly for a while, letting in strong rays of dust-filled light across the near-empty reading tables, then the skies darkened again, bringing more and heavier rains down on the white stucco building around him.

Several times Toland had all three books open simultaneously, referencing each against the other on this or that major point. Twice he got up and went to the rows of encyclopedias located near the entrance of the south wing, extracted a selected volume, checked it, then came back to continue reading.

Once, he unconsciously removed his pipe and pouch from inside his white coat, but before he had a chance to light up, the same trim librarian with the Oriental eyes tapped him on his shoulder, leaned down and quietly said, "That's a no-no!"

Toland looked up from his pipe, smiled back at the grinning young woman, then went back to his reading.

The rain continued coming down outside, then finally died, but the afternoon remained gray, and dull shadows were cast across his table as he closed the last book. For a long moment he stared into the empty space in front of him. Then he got up, placed each book back in its proper slot, and departed.

From the top step Toland glanced over at the black-faced clock in the church steeple across the street. It read 4:25. He'd had enough history for one day, and Cho, if he was still living in Honolulu, would be setting up the tables in Soochow's about then anyway. With his paper bag tucked under his arm, and feeling free to smoke now, he cupped the lighted match and began pulling on his pipe while moving down the steps.

Toland never considered himself any more clumsy or awkward than the next man, but doubt had crept in his mind lately as to his ability to be considerate of his fellow man. So, when the middleaged woman's books fell from her arms and into a scatter down the wet steps, one landing squarely in a rain puddle at the bottom, and hearing her angry voice saying, "Why can't you Navy people watch where you're going!" he immediately felt completely responsible for the apparent collision. He really was not watching where he was going.

She continued speaking in a demanding tone as Toland, disregarding his own small bundle that had fallen to the fourth wet step, retrieved each of the five books, including the one at the bottom. He attempted to shake it free of the rain water. It was a murder mystery written by Agatha Christie.

"You Navy people are just everywhere. Up the streets, down the streets. Everywhere I go, there you are. Don't you ever stay on your ships?"

"Yes, ma'am."

"No, you don't! I see you sailors everywhere I go." Then, as Toland carried her books in one arm and pushed back the brass door leading back into the lower foyer of the library with the other, she added, "You officers seem nice enough I guess, but its all your sailors making such a shambles of our beautiful Honolulu, and our sweet girls. It's a sin and shame, that's what it is. And I'm going to write our Mr. Poindexter about it!"

"Yes, ma'am."

The Oriental librarian rescued the books from Toland's arms while courteously greeting the woman by name.

Back on the steps, Toland looked around, then picked up his wet brown sack and was about to continue on down the rest of the steps when the young woman called after him.

He stopped and looked back as she said, with no trace of an Oriental accent, "I watched the whole thing from that window, Chief. You never even touched her. That old bitch, she just tripped. Over her own tongue, I think."

It didn't appear to Toland that the rain would commence again for awhile so he began walking the eight blocks back to River Street.

On the premise that man does eternally seek truth and wishes ultimately to find ways in which to get along with himself rather than to destroy himself, then the responsibility of reading history and writing history is twofold. There will always be those who will wish to slant the recordings of history to their own political, racial, or religious points of view, sometimes even at the expense of their own country's honest efforts and goals. However, with the passing of time the slanters grow louder but their numbers are relatively fewer. The recorders of history, on the other hand, find less and less room to corrupt it. Their works are an open book, so to speak, and subject to more careful and wider scrutiny, not only from the reference seekers but from their own contemporaries. They must be objective to stay in the business, science, or art of being responsible historians. Therefore their errors, which nevertheless still occur, are more often minor in nature rather than major, and more often human rather than deliberate. If one is to weigh the conscientious responsibilities of the reader against the writer of history, then it must be the reader owing the greater degree of responsibility, as it is he who will form opinions, act upon them, and shape further history. In the beginning he needs only to cross reference.

These were the facts as far as Toland could conscientiously discover in a short time:

In 1894, and without a declaration of war, a squadron of Japanese warships attacked without warning a Chinese force of ships, carrying troops to Korea to put down a rebellion in that country. A declared war between China and Japan followed in which Japan virtually wiped out the Chinese Navy and defeated her forces on land. She won the war and with it the Leatung Peninsula and the island of Formosa. Shortly thereafter, a government oriented to Japan's needs was set up in Korea, and a Japanese occupation force was installed. In 1910, Korea was formally annexed to Japan and promptly renamed Chosen.

At midnight, Monday, February 8, 1904, again without

warning or declaration of war, the Japanese Fleet stood outside the entrance to Port Arthur and sent in a flotilla of torpedo boats. They sank a Russian cruiser anchored in the center of the harbor and torpedoed and forced to beach two Russian first-class battleships. The torpedo boats escaped unharmed. As reported, many of the officers and men of the Russian Fleet were ashore in places of amusement. A declared war followed in which Japan was victorious on land as well as at sea. Her prize for winning that war, in addition to Port Arthur and Dairen, was a large portion of southern Manchuria.

In August, 1914, and again without warning or declaration of war, a Japanese Fleet blockaded Tsingtao in Shantung Province, then declared war against Germany and attacked her naval vessels in and around the harbor. She seized most of Germany's island possessions in the Pacific.

On September 18, 1931, the so-called Mukden Incident occurred, in which Japanese troops attacked without warning and overran the rest of Manchuria. China protested to the League of Nations, but to no avail. Manchuria was shortly thereafter renamed Manchukuo. Japan then had control of the whole of upper China.

Moving south now, with her eyes on the rich commerce trade routes leading from southern China to all parts of the world with ships carrying oil, tin, rubber, and other valuable goods, Japan found reasons for indiscriminately bombing cities and landing her marines to protect her 'interests,' most notably Shanghai, in January 1932.

Then, on the night of July 7, 1937, in Peiping, at the old Marco Polo Bridge northwest of the city and near the end of the ancient Great Wall of China, Japan without warning or declaration of war launched her final solution to the 'China Problem' by invading the whole of China for complete East Asian conquest. Japan then presented to the world a bloody example of what unrestrained military activities can produce in a country, culminating as it did in "The Rape of Nanking."

She seemed intoxicated with her victories, never knowing defeat. But Indochina had to be next if she were to grease her conquests. So, on September 22, 1940, without provocation, warning, or declaration of war, Japan invaded French Indochina.

And, now, very likely an attack on the Philippines would follow. Who was there to stop her? The Western powers were all preoccupied with Adolph Hitler and his conquests.

As he turned off River Street onto Pauhai and walked a few yards down, Toland saw the familiar red and black sign reaching out over the sidewalk and hung by what appeared to be two golden dragons—"Soochow's."

Leaving behind the multitude of late afternoon Oriental shoppers and sidewalk merchants, Toland parted the strings of beads and stepped into the cool establishment. A strong whiff of disinfectant mixed with incense indicated the place had been swabbed down and made ready for the weekend crowds that would be wandering in shortly. The lights had not been turned low yet, and he could see the chairs were down and in place, and a young shapely girl with a slit up the side of her skirt all the way to her slender waist moving about and lighting the little candles in the center of each table. The bar already had two or three early guests.

It had been five years since Toland had been in here, but it still looked the same, a little smaller maybe but the same green and red paper lanterns hung in their original places from the black-painted overhead. He half doubted he would find his friend, Cho, still there. After all, he was only a head cook before, maybe a part owner. And five years is a long time. So the surprise was pleasant when he caught sight of, and approached his aging friend in a large fanback chair over near the double doors that led into the kitchen. He was leaning forward, napkin in place at his chin, and working chopsticks through his rice in a green crock bowl.

Toland put his hand on Cho's table and shook it a little. The two men stared at each other a moment, then the Chinaman said, "Ah, Earl-son. You Chief-son! You sonamagun!"

"Four years ago, Cho. How've you been?"

Without getting up, the heavyset man reached for a chair from the next table over and pulled it in place for Toland. After he was seated, Cho put an arm over his friend and shook both of Toland's hands with his other.

"How come you neva come back see you buddy Cho? Where you been long time?"

"Here and there, Cho, here and there. Who's the number one cook in Honolulu, Cho?"

"Not me Earl-son," he said indignantly. Then, with a greasy grin while sweeping his free arm around the room, "I now own this ho' house of sin." Then to prove his point he shouted several words in Chinese toward the bar, and another maid with a similar slit up the side of her skirt bowed respectfully and with a smile hurried off into the kitchen.

"Well, you moved up, Cho. That's good!"

"Course I move up. You move up too, Chief-son. Nobody stay same for long. Either move up or down, no stay same, 'cept friendship. Right? Now you share rice bowl with you ole buddy Cho."

The two old friends swapped some small talk, and the young woman brought over two more steaming bowls of brown rice with green seasoning sprinkled on top. Without looking up, the two men continued speaking to each other while putting it away. At one point Toland aimed one of his chopsticks at Cho's large belly, commenting on it having enjoyed good rice over the years. Cho laughed and returned the remark, aimed at Toland's trim stomach which to him had not been having the same.

Then the Oriental was reminded of their last game together, of which Toland had been the winner. Cho clapped his hands and spoke more words in his native language, and the chess board was brought over along with the small cherrywood box. As the young black-haired woman began setting up the pieces in front of them, Cho slipped his hand under the slit of her skirt and patted her bottom.

"This a Mi Ling! You likey, Earl-son? I fixy you up later to—"

Before he could finish 'tonight,' the shapely young Chinese girl slapped the top of his balding head, not as hard as she could have, but enough so that it must have stung a little.

"Earl-son can speak for Earl-son," she said, continuing to smile, "the great Cho speak only for Cho."

Toland sat back in his chair and laughed at his friend, who while rubbing his head, said, "Everybody edgy in Honolulu these days." Then he winked at Toland.

Toland began his game with the black ivory pieces, while Cho, after winning the white from the girl's outstretched hands, started the game off with the standard king-pawn-four. He gained good position early and held onto it, costing Toland a bishop and pawn by the middle of the game. Twenty minutes later, with only his king and rook left to Cho's king, queen, and one pawn, Toland conceded the game, while his chess opponent beamed with victory.

Before the second game began, in which Toland would now have the white, Cho without speaking noticed the brown paper bag resting at Toland's right elbow. The Chief glanced at it too and remembered he should be calling his friend, Mace.

Begging off for a moment, Toland went to the pay phone near the beaded entrance, dropped a nickel in the slot, and dialed the number that Mace had scribbled off earlier. An elderly gentleman's voice answered after the third ring, and Toland asked him to let Chief Mace know that he had called and would be out to see him tomorrow. Then he thanked him for relaying the message, which the gentleman politely promised to do.

Returning to Cho and the chess pieces, all set up for a replay, Toland reached for the sack. And with grandeur he removed the bright silk but slightly wrinkled sport shirt, to which his Chinese friend and two bar maids applauded in great approval. Toland then extracted a five-dollar bill from his wallet, dropped it in front of his Oriental friend, and then and there began removing his clothing as far down as his white trousers. One of the giggling girls began carefully folding and stacking each garment as he tossed it on the table.

"You sonamagun, same funny fellow, long time no see. Tonight you no pay. On my house of sin!" He spoke again in Chinese to the girl handling the chief's clothing, and with Toland's white cap on top of her head, she politely bowed then scurried off behind another beaded curtain near the small bandstand opposite the bar. Toland, now more comfortable in his sport shirt and white pants, settled down to beat his Oriental friend at the royal game of chess, in spite of his having had little chance to practice in the past few years.

Soochow's began to fill up. Several girls had already arrived in small groups and had changed into their scanty costumes for the evening, taking up stations along the bar. A few lingered or swayed just outside the beaded entrance, to a Glenn Miller recording being piped through a speaker that hung from the red-and-black sign over the sidewalk. The music and girls combined to draw wandering servicemen into Cho's establishment of 'sin.'

Shortly before eight o'clock, three black musicians climbed onto the small bandstand and began tuning and warming up for the all-night crowd that was expected, one on the trumpet the other two on piano and drums.

Except for a shaded lamp over their table, ordered by Cho earlier, the lights inside had long since dimmed and the crowd had filled to a overflowing capacity before the chubby Oriental finally conceded the game. Cho was down to his king and one knight to Toland's king and two rooks, and one unavoidable move away from a checkmate. Toland had had three bourbon highballs by then and was glad the game was over, and he got an unexpected giggling kiss on the cheek from Mi Ling.

"We play again tomorrow, you sonamagun!" laughed Cho, good-naturedly. "And I fixy you good steak." At that moment one of the large Chinese bouncers came over, whispered something in Cho's ear, then the overweight proprietor pushed back the table, arose, and departed through the crowd around him.

With the board and chess pieces removed from the table and two fresh drinks set before them, Toland glanced around at the crowd. He listened to the wild laughter and applause given the jazz group as they finished up on their jump version of 'Hong Kong Blues,' and then they went right into 'Sophisticated Lady.' Mi Ling appeared very small indeed in the large fanbacked chair previously occupied by Cho.

"You likey Mi Ling, Chief-son?"

Toland smiled back, and said, "Sure, I likey." Then he gulped down half the contents of the glass, and said, "Come on, let's try it!"

On the crowded floor there was no real room to dance, just enough for a little movement to the left and right.

Being very close and looking down into her almost innocent young face, he tried to figure out why he was perspiring so much and she was not. Then he told her she was a very good dancer, and she genuinely laughed with glee, as they were hardly dancing at all. And then he laughed along with her.

They had only one more drink together, tried one more dance on the floor, then he asked her where she had taken his clothes.

"Come on. I show you!" She answered. Then she led the way through the crowd, and on through the beaded curtain next to the blaring bandstand, down the hall a few steps, and then they began climbing the stairs together.

Halfway up the dimly-lit staircase, Toland stumbled then stopped. He looked squarely into Mi Ling's soft pleasant face, and asked, "Have you ever been sunk at Port Arthur!"

"Port Arthur?" she repeated.

"Yeah, Port Arthur. North China."

"I am Cantonese girl," she proudly beamed, "from South China!"

"That's the best kind, ma'am. You are a southern Chinese Belle!"

"I am southern Chinese, bell?"

They both laughed at each other. Then their eyes met straight on, and with their sudden awareness of each other's presence Toland reached down and swallowed her small, willing figure in his arms. After a few moments they continued on up the darkened staircase.

He thought romantically about carrying her the rest of the way, but she was at least a step ahead of him at that point.

CHAPTER VI

"WHAT THE HELL
KIND OF PLACE IS THIS ANYWAY!"

The midmorning sun warmed Toland's bare back as he leaned over the wrought-iron balcony railing just above the red and black sign to scan the throngs of Oriental merchants and shoppers below for some familiar face. He was without clothing except for his white scivvy shorts. A few people glanced up at him from the crowd below, some of them women, and they giggled. Toland waved back at one of them, then realizing his almost nude condition began pulling back inside, but just then he caught sight of Mi Ling hurrying through the crowd from down the street. And with his freshly laundered clothes in one arm, she laughingly waved back to him with her other.

After they played on the rumpled bed together for a few more minutes, Toland got his white shoes and pants on, and, foregoing his white shirt and coat, he decided to spend the rest of the day in Mace's bright silk sport shirt. Breakfast served to them consisted of ham, scrambled eggs, and fried bananas.

"I got to see a buddy," he answered her pouting face.

"You come back see Mi Ling?" she asked sweetly.

"Sure, I'll be back," he said with a smile and, pointing over at his clothes, "You got my gear there don't you?"

She hugged him close a moment, then let him go. Looking down into her warm face, he wanted to say a lot of things. That he was old enough to be her father, for one.

That she made him feel worthwhile again, for another. And he wanted to say there really wasn't any 'buddy' in the world who was worth any length of his time that could compare to just one moment with her. But all he did was smile back at her, and then he left.

On the street below Toland darted through the crowd, flagged down an approaching cab, and climbed in. As the taxi left the curb, the chief put his arm out through the open window and waved back at Mi Ling who he knew would be waving down from the balcony above.

Having given his orders to the driver, Toland settled back for the long ride through town, up over the Pali, and down the northeastern side of the island, to the little village of Kaneohe. He could have been thinking of Mi Ling, or the steak and rematch his good friend Cho promised and wanted, but he wasn't. He spent most of the time thinking of his two children. Among other things, he seriously thought of what he might send them for Christmas. Mace was right. If he wanted to get them something, he would have to mail it off soon to get there in time.

The cabby didn't bother to get out. He just put on his brakes in front of some kids out in the street who were playing catch with a football. "That'll be a buck-ten, friend."

Toland got out and handed him the exact change through the open window, just as the football bounced off the running board of the cab and wobbled still at Toland's feet.

The driver backed the cab around and drove off in the direction he had just come as Toland, sticking a few coins back in his pocket, picked up the ball and tossed it in the air a couple of times. As he started to throw it back he noticed they weren't kids at all. At least, one of them wasn't. The nearest one was a slender woman in boys' jeans about ten years younger than himself. She was wearing a cap, and with a half smile she patiently waited for Toland to toss her the ball. On the other side of her and up a few yards a boy of about twelve and a girl with the same laughing face in the picture back in Mace's radio shack waited, too.

Toland overthrew the waiting woman, and the boy made a fine leaping catch for the ball. The woman did not return Toland's wink.

The potted asphalt street was on a slight decline going downhill, and on either side were almost identical small bungalows of various colors. Some were just a little better kept than others. Each was mounted on cement blocks about three feet off the ground, and one could easily see under and clear through to the back yards where heavy tropical foliage was growing. A few old automobiles were parked in the dirt driveways.

Looking around for the right address, Toland glanced at a small dog being chased by a large cat under a house to his left, heard a screen door open and slam to his right, then saw Mace on the porch tucking his shirt in his pants and smiling broadly. "Hey, Earl you old son of a gun, why didn't you call? I'd have come down to pick you up. Come on in!"

Toland waved back at his friend, glanced once more at the slender woman who now had the ball, then climbed the wooden steps and followed Mace back inside.

Mace talked about the rain they'd had yesterday afternoon and how it seemed to flood everything on their block.

Passing through the small living room that had the appearance of a place someone was trying to keep cozy and neat, Toland noticed in the corner of the frayed overstuffed couch a red and blue satin pillow with the words 'San Diego' written across the front of it. And on the main wall high and in the center, a large blown-up tinted wedding photo of Mace, stiff-faced in his dress blues, with his wife smiling back beside him. A lot of knick-knacks, mostly sea shells, adorned the small coffee table and window sills around the room.

Now in the kitchen, Mace directed his friend to sit at the

chrome-legged table while he removed two cans of beer from the top of the icebox, then glanced back in to see how much ice was left.

He continued talking about the rain and the mud, then cussed at the Red Cross people for claiming in the paper to have helped the folks at the far end of his street who were flooded out. "Hell, they said they would come back later and inoculate the kids in the neighborhood or something, and that's the last we heard of them. Now they take all the credit and want another donation drive. The fact is, me and a bunch of guys went down there again this morning, helped them get cleaned up, and gave them some of our own gear."

Toland stood up as the chief radioman's wife, wearing a nervous smile, stepped into the kitchen in a freshly ironed cotton print dress. She hesitated a moment, not knowing whether to offer her hand to Toland or not. Toland put her at ease by reaching over and gently taking her hand for a moment. Then he sat back down.

"Ya see, Doris, isn't he just like I told ya? Good-looking guy, too, ain't he!"

Toland knew there wasn't anything good looking about himself, and knew the remark embarrassed Mace's wife.

"Oh, Charlie," she said, "maybe Mr. Toland would rather have some coffee than that beer. I'll put on a fresh pot."

"That's OK, Mrs. Mace, the beer will be fine," said Toland.

"I'm going to put a fresh pot on anyway, just in case," she answered.

"What's this Mr. Toland and Mrs. Mace business? He's Earl, you're Doris, and I'm Charlie. But God, how I hate the name Charlie."

Everybody laughed a moment, then Doris said again, "Oh, Charlie, I love it. You remember that old song Mr. Toland, I mean Earl, 'Oh Charlie Oh'." Then she began to sing it, substituting the name 'Charlie' for 'Johnny', and

Toland joined in to humor her while Mace quietly put his head in his hand and patiently listened. Then, good-naturedly, he reached over and swatted her on the bottom, and everybody laughed some more.

The screen door opened, and shut with a bang and the little girl of five or six, who had been playing catch in the street ran through the living room and kitchen and landed in her father's lap, pouting terribly. Mace proudly introduced her as his Cathy, then asked the little girl, "What's wrong now, sugar!"

"It's Donny! When it's my turn to catch the ball, Verna throws it to me, only Donny jumps over and catches it every time." And then she buried her face in her father's arms.

Mace hugged his young daughter and pacified her with, "Donny probably was only practicing interceptions, honey."

Smiling at her Charlie, Doris said to Toland, "Verna's the girl next door. She was the one who came over and said you'd called last night. She and her little boy live with her dad. He's a preacher."

"He's not a preacher!" said Mace, "He's a missionary I keep tellin' ya," and, turning to Toland, "at least he was. They're Seventh-day Adventist, but real nice people. Anyway, last June just before Doris and the kids came over from the States he was in a plane carrying a lot of supplies over to Molokai when the plane crashed on take off. Got his back and shoulder banged up, and—"

"Let me tell the rest, Charlie. Anyway, Verna—that's his daughter—her husband died or something right after Donald was born, and when old Mr. Walker got hurt in that plane crash she and Donald came over on the same boat we did. We got to be good friends, and we went house-hunting together. Charlie didn't want us living in that old Navy Housing, anyway."

Toland took another sip of his beer and tried to appear interested as Doris made one more comment, about the woman working in a dentist's office downtown, then a knock came on the screen door and it opened again.

From the living room Toland overheard Doris urging Verna, who had just made an apology for her son's possible selfishness, to come into the kitchen and meet Charlie's best friend from the *Nevada*. She declined on the pretense that she didn't look presentable. A few more words were spoken, then the screen door opened, and closed, then Doris returned to the kitchen alone, but she was wearing a curious smile.

Later that afternoon, while Doris prepared a chicken dinner, Toland in an old pair of dungarees lent to him by Mace helped his friend pull out the dashboard from his old Studebaker, to fix the speedometer cable and work on the horn that hadn't sounded since he purchased the car some weeks earlier. While they were laboring at it, Mace explained he had got a good deal on 'her' from a Marine Staff Sergeant who was to be transferred back to the States and was forced to sell. "Only I still keep seeing him pullin' guard duty around the Main Gate. He told me he was getting transferred right away. You think he was shittin' me, Earl?"

An hour or so later, with the dashboard back in place again, they started her up and went for a drive back down on the coast highway. The speedometer still didn't work, but the horn sounded fine for the first time, and together they laughed, each of them pressing on it several times just to make sure.

On the way back home Mace slowed down and stopped for two young boys walking along the windy highway. The larger one was carrying a cardboard grocery box full of assorted beach objects.

Now in the car, the oldest boy of fourteen or so excitedly brought from the box a large green glass ball with thick knotted twine wrapped around it. The twine was still wet.

"Hey, Dad, look what we found. Isn't it a beauty? It washed up on the beach right where we were hunting."

"Yeah, son, a Japanese fishing float. They break loose from their fishing nets and float all over the Pacific, sometimes farther than that."

"Is it worth anything, Dad?"

"That one looks like it is," answered Mace, shifting into low and driving off again. He introduced Toland to his oldest child, Leon, and then reaching back shook the hair of Donald, who had left the game of catching football to hunt for shells with his next door friend. Donald, recognizing Toland as the one who had thrown him the ball earlier, winked back at him now sitting up front.

After dinner Mace and Toland took their coffee into the small living room while Doris and Leon cleared the table and began doing the dishes, with an honest assist from Cathy. The men talked about more old times and were a little more detailed on their separate past experiences, as Leon and Cathy quietly listened from the kitchen doorway. Later, Doris came in with the children and, discarding the damp dish towel for the worn photo album from under the coffee table, proudly began showing her family's growth and activities over the years. There was an occasional picture of herself playing an accordion, and one old shot of her in a group of high school students taken, she explained, before she met Mace. The children pleaded, and then with a little coaxing from Mace and Toland she went into the bedroom and came out with her old but still shiny black and white accordian. Mace helped her get strapped in, and in a little while they were all singing the old songs. She and her choral group around her were best on 'Red Sails in the Sunset'.

Toland spent the night on their couch, and the next morning slept while the others quietly moved around him from the bathroom to the kitchen. There, Doris was preparing a nice breakfast for her family and their guest.

They packed a picnic, and the day was spent driving completely around the island of Oahu, staying mostly along the shore. Reaching the northwest end of the island, they stopped and had their lunch at Waimea Beach, and after cleaning up their litter, they tossed the football around in the wet sand near the surf. Then back in the car and while driving on Mace pointed out to Toland a few of the new radar installations that had gone up around the island recently.

It was dark by the time they reached home again. Toland declined the offer of a late dinner, and another invitation to spend one more night. Before getting back in the car for the trip into town, as Mace insisted on driving him, Toland found an opportunity to give Leon the five-dollar bill, to be put in his mother's purse. He made the boy promise that he wouldn't mention this to his father.

The ride from Kaneohe Bay and back over the Pali to the glittering lights of the city below was spent mostly in silence between the two men. They smiled at each other and shook hands just before Toland left the car at the familiar intersection of Punch Bowl and King streets. Toland lied as he explained, "No, that's OK. I got my gear in a locker club right around the corner."

"Then I'll wait and drive ya' to the Main Gate."

"No, I said. Anyway I'm going to spend a couple hours in town before going back to the ship."

"OK. But I want you to know me and Doris and the kids—"

"Don't say it, man. It was all my pleasure. And you're real lucky, ya got a real nice family there."

"OK, buddy. See ya at quarters in the morning."

After his friend left the curb, Toland crossed the street and headed for Soochow's.

Even for a Sunday night, and a day away from payday there were still a few servicemen out walking the streets, mostly in small groups moving in and out of the joints and dives along King and Hotel while the B girls out front did their best to coax them all into their place.

Toland walked into Soochow's and, without looking around, continued on through the sparsely occupied tables and over to the little opening next to the bandstand. Parting the strings of beads, he then made his way down the dimly lit hall and climbed the steps two at a time to the second floor. Without knocking, he entered the dark, stale bedroom, and immediately knew he was not alone. A neon sign flashed off and on from a bar across the street, and enough light came in so he could make out the portable cardboard closet he had seen standing in the corner earlier, and where he hoped to find his clothes.

With his hopes and guess realized to be true, and while ignoring the occupants in the bed over near the louvered door leading onto the balcony, he at once began removing his sport shirt and changing into the rest of his white uniform. A few inaudible words were spoken from the bed, then clearly the words, "Son of a bitch!" came across to Toland who was hurrying as fast as he could, more out of sympathy for the occupants than of any fear of them.

"Relax, buddy. I'll be out in a minute."

"I'm going to bust you out on your ass, wise guy!"

Ignoring the threat, Toland continued getting into his uniform, and then began looking around for the brown paper bag, then thought, 'the hell with it.' He had the door open again and was halfway through when he heard the voice of Mi Ling behind him, then felt a hand grab for his shoulder. The chief automatically moved to one side as the man's other arm with a fist on the end brushed by his head. Toland grabbed the arm and pulled it against the door jamb and said, "I told ya to relax! Now go on back and enjoy life."

In her robe and halfway down the stairs Mi Ling caught up with Toland and angrily cursed him in Chinese. He reached in his pockets and pulled out all the money he had left, three dollars and seventy cents. He kept the twenty cents for a cup of coffee and bus ride back to Pearl and shoved the rest in her hands, saying, "Tell Cho I'll be back for that steak and chess game later," then he smiled at her.

She almost threw the money back in his face, but didn't. Instead she wrinkled up her chin and with pressed lips managed a small smile, while the man, nursing his sore arm back up in the doorway, shouted down his demand to know, "What the hell kind of place is this anyway?"

At 0745, Monday, November 10, Quarters for Muster and Inspection were sounded on board almost every Naval vessel throughout the harbor. Some ships had already weighed anchor or left their moorings and berths and were underway for another week of local operations. The old battleship *Utah* scheduled in this week's events proudly moved out to sea to join her sisters, but she would figure only from a 'target' point of view.

Nevada, securely tied to Ten-Ten Dock, exercised fair weather parade as a dozen or so divisions in groups of forty to sixty men lined her weather decks to be inspected, counted, and to receive the working Plan-Of-The-Day.

Operations recorded no absentees. Then Chief Gonza, with Chiefs Toland, Mace, and Simpson to his left, rattled off the POD to the men before him at parade rest, inserting commands of his own from time to time, bringing to their attention the deficient or slack conditions existing within the division, which he had made note of during the preceding week. Occasionally the assistant division officer, Mr. Lord at his right, whispered a comment near Gonza's ear; then more commands were made. A strong reference concerning the bridge urinal was made, even though no one but commissioned officers were allowed to use it.

Lieutenant Commander Morgan approached his division just as "First Call" was sounded. The men were brought respectfully to attention, salutes were made and returned, and after Morgan directed the men to be put at ease, he congratulated them for their efforts of the past week and then announced, "Captain's Mast will be held for Shadd at 1300."

Eight bells were sounded promptly at 0800, and immediately following colors the word was passed, "Turn to! Continue ship's work, carry out the Plan-Of-the-Day."

The week went by fast and happily for most of the crew. Shadd received a bust from Third Class Yeoman down to Seaman but remained in the division. The additional sentence of fifteen days in the brig and forfeiture of a month's pay was suspended due to his clean record and to the fact that this was his first offense.

Pay call was held Monday afternoon as scheduled, and Chief Gonza was involved in two lines—one in which he received his own pay and the other in which he had a man stationed at the end of the crew's pay line on the mess decks to receive or lend additional sums of money through his slush fund.

Near the end of the week Gonza was again feeling the other chiefs out for a standby. He had had the duty the previous Friday. Now he was faced with the duty for the upcoming Saturday and Sunday. Weekday standbys were not difficult to arrange, but it was the weekends that most men valued. Thursday afternoon, Mace was furious when he heard the news that Toland had consented to swap weekends with Gonza.

"What the hell did you do that for, Earl? Doris and me had something really planned for this weekend, which included you."

"The fact is, buddy," Toland said, taking another bite of his early supper and just before going on watch, "I've been able to get a lot of chart and pub work out of the way because of Brock and Pollard. Gonza did make them available to me, and I owe him for that."

"You don't owe that bastard nothing. How do you think them charts got in that shape in the first place?"

Toland continued eating, then Mace said, "What am I going to tell Doris? She was really counting on you. You know how women are with them plans of theirs!"

Toland bit his upper lip a moment, then said, "Look, buddy, I'm sorry, but that's the way it is. Let's make it another weekend. I won't have a duty weekend for over a month." Then he smiled and added, "You got a nice wife there. You're real lucky, ya know that?"

"I know, you said that already. But you haven't seen her when she's mad."

A half hour later, Mace crossed over the enlisted Quarterdeck on his way home, but before departing he had a few more words with Toland who now had the gangway watch, his regularly scheduled evening of duty.

"Well, she's going to be mad, Earl. But she'll figure something out."

"They always do, buddy," answered Toland, "they always do!"

"Request permission to leave the ship!"

"Permission granted!"

After the exchange of salutes, Toland watched his friend move down the gangway, wave back once more, then disappear in the evening crowds of sailors on their way to what they hoped would be an enjoyable evening in town.

Most of the 1600 to 2000 watch was over, and all that were going ashore had departed *Nevada* some time earlier. Toland was glad he didn't have either of the next two watches as they were the ones where several of *Nevada*'s sailors would be ordered or escorted back to their ship because of misconduct, ranging from simple out-of-uniform to being drunk and disorderly. And each case had to be properly recorded in the log. It was always a headache.

Toland turned to his messenger and was about to tell him to lay below and check on the reliefs, when he noticed Slaughter had a fixed gaze on the signal tower sending out a routine light message to the dry-docked *Pennsylvania* up ahead. It was obvious the young sailor was having some difficulty making out the words.

"You know the Morse Code OK?"

"Sure I do, Chief, but sometimes it just goes too fast for

me. And Chief Gonza ain't gonna' give me another chance unless I can get it better by Monday."

"All right, let's try it again. He's sending something different now. This time think about this for a second. You can't read a book or newspaper letter for letter and expect to get anywhere. You got to read it word for word. Ya follow me?"

"Got ya!"

"OK, now I'll read it word for word and you concentrate on the way I told you. — won't — put — out — but — Sonja — he's spelling Sonja again, did ya get that? —Sonja — will — X — having — party — her — place — at —.Now he's sending numerals. Probably the address. Numerals are a little more tricky than—"

"Get the numerals, Chief. Good God!"

"Get your ass below and get the reliefs. Now!"

"Right, Chief. I'm on my way, but if you could—"

"Get going!"

Friday was another fast day. Toland and his small crew nearly had the charts and new file up to date and ready for any inspection that might come along. One was scheduled in mid-January, an 'Admin'. He would be prepared for it, he felt sure.

The duty section mustered on Saturday morning, and afterward Toland made the rounds in the areas of his responsibility. Then in the proper uniform assumed the morning-to-noon watch on the forward Quarterdeck, as previously scheduled for Gonza.

By 1100 a few of the crew's guests began to arrive for dinner and Toland courteously welcomed them aboard, then had the word passed below decks for the specific sailor who may or may not have been expecting their arrival. But it was the officer's gangway aft that Toland noticed was getting the most visitors and attention. Their women were certainly nice looking, and dressed very well for the occasion. Then his eyes caught sight of a family of visitors coming around the north end of Ship Repair Building Eight, and heading for *Nevada*, and Toland's own Quarterdeck: three children, two women, and a man. The man, in a bright-colored sport shirt, waved an arm, then herded a little girl back with his group and continued coming on. It was Mace.

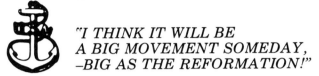

CHAPTER VII

"I THINK IT WILL BE A BIG MOVEMENT SOMEDAY, –BIG AS THE REFORMATION!"

Toland flushed red and was embarrassed for a moment. Then as the group drew nearer he began to feel better about it, then better still as both women were neatly dressed and looked very trim, possibly in their Sunday best. The chief quartermaster looked down the line to the officer's gangway and thought he saw a few admiring glances being cast in the direction of Mace's family.

Without looking directly into the passing faces of Doris and Verna, Toland nevertheless managed a smile as he saluted the boarding party. Going by, Doris said quietly, "You wouldn't come to us, so we came to you." The nicely dressed children laughed and giggled as they went by. Donald would not continue until he got his salute, then came on. Bringing up the rear and shrugging his round shoulders, Mace said with a smile, "Well, I told ya she'd think of something!"

About fifteen minutes later Toland was relieved by the oncoming watch and then hesitantly he joined Mace and his guests in the chiefs' mess below.

Conveniently following lunch, an afternoon movie was shown on the crew's mess decks. Not *Gulliver's Travels* as one might have hoped, but interesting enough, as it turned out, to occupy the children for a couple of hours, especially Cathy: six reels of Bette Davis and George Brent, in *Jezebel*.

While Charlie entertained his Doris in the radio room one deck below, Toland overcame his awkwardness and made an attempt at explaining the various objects and instruments around the wheelhouse to Verna.

Watching her walk around the bridge, mostly with her back to him, Toland couldn't help noticing that the tight bun of hair behind her small head had begun to slip a little. It was now being loosely held in place by a few simple hairpins. In a moment she reached back and pressed them in more firmly, then, raising up on her tip toes and peering over the massive ship's wheel, she asked if he steered the ship. He answered no, that it generally wasn't expected of him.

Still looking over the wheel and not at Toland, she said, "I think Doris and Charlie had something in mind for us." Then she added, "Anyway, I'm just glad Donald had a chance to come down on the boat today. He's wanted to for such a long time now."

With a partial smile and almost defensively she turned and looked directly at Toland and asked, "Are you sorry we came?"

Now Toland noticed her, really, for the first time. She wasn't a beautiful woman as the word generally implies, and if it were not for the small amount of makeup she wore on her mouth and cheeks one might have thought she was rather plain. But in her large brown eyes there seemed to be a kind of private little mystery, one she might even like to share, perhaps with the right someone.

Toland removed one of his hands that had been resting in his back pocket, reached up and pulled at his ear lobe, and said, "Why the heck did you say that?" Then he added, without giving her a chance to reply, "Listen, when the movie's over, we'll take Donald all over this rust bucket if he wants. But some places you'll have to stay outside."

She quickly put one hand to her mouth and gave a relaxed laugh. And they both laughed together.

Out on the starboard wing and in full view of the harbor

they talked with a little more ease. The chief quartermaster answered her simple questions as to the purpose of this ship and that ship. At one point he left her alone for a moment, just long enough to go below to his charthouse and return with two mugs of hot coffee. And she seemed as delighted at the refreshment as she was with his attention to her. Then they discussed the possibility of later having a date together, just to show Doris and Charlie they were not antisocial. Maybe dinner in a place with some nice atmosphere. "I know just," they both spoke at once.

Toland admitted he had no automobile. Verna, on the other hand, stated she was making small payments on a 1936 Pontiac coupé. Then, true to his word, when the movie was over he gave her anxious boy a tour of *Nevada* from stem to stern, with his delighted mother trailing not far behind. Though he didn't mention it, most of the spaces they visited Toland, himself, had not entered since coming aboard. There hadn't been any need or time for it until now.

Finally returning to the CPO wardroom, they found Mace and his family enjoying a kind of lumpy chocolate ge-dunk made up by the duty mess cooks, and Toland got down three more saucers. At the mess table Mace and Toland had fun telling the youngsters that in the Navy ice cream is always referred to as "ge-dunk" and candy as "poggy bait." The reasons were not explained.

And then Doris mentioned to Charlie that Thanksgiving was coming up on next Thursday.

"Of course he's gonna come," said Mace, "if he don't get big and decide to standby for somebody again."

"We decided to fix dinner at Verna's," Doris said, happily. "She's got a bigger table, and her Dad don't have to walk so far."

Toland looked from Verna's agreeable face to glance across the table at Donald, who had stopped eating his dessert. The boy winked at Toland, and Toland winked back in affirmative.

The following day, finishing out the duty weekend, Toland arose and showered around 0730. On his way to breakfast he passed a couple of duty bandsmen with their shiny brass instruments who had just come in from playing the National Anthem on the fantail. Then he spent most of the morning listening to a broadcast of the Cleveland Rams battling it out with the Detroit Lions back in the States.

Chief Darnell didn't have the duty, but he was aboard anyway seeing about his engines. He came up in time for lunch and declared *Nevada* would be ready for sea in two weeks, the time it would take for a couple of parts to be ordered and flown out from the Fore River Shipbuilding Company on the East Coast where she had been built. Then Darnell asked what the final score was. Someone answered, "Detroit! 28 to 17."

During the course of lunch Toland offhandedly asked the chief machinist mate what *Nevada*'s estimated radius of action was.

He thought a moment, then asked, "At full speed, twenty knots?"

"Yes, full speed," Toland said.

"About 4,000 miles. Maybe 4,500 in good seas."

Following lunch Toland made the rounds of his spaces again, came back to the CPO mess tables, and after a challenge played three games of acey-deucy, in which he lost all three. When he wasn't thinking of Verna, he was thinking of oilers.

The next three days passed quickly, and Wednesday afternoon Mace came into the chartroom to remind Toland that it was getting late and they should go below and start getting cleaned up before leaving the ship.

The prospect of spending another night on Mace's couch wasn't an altogether appealing thought to Toland, and anyway *Nevada*'s own cooks were in the process of preparing a mighty fine Thanksgiving feast for her crew, to which Mace and his family and guests were all welcome to attend if they wished. And it would save a lot of work for the women. But Toland waved back at his departing friend, in assurance that he would be along shortly.

Climbing the middle ladder, the chief quartermaster reached the wheelhouse just as Mickey Harris stepped in from the port wing carrying a noticeably bulging substance under his blue denim shirt, which ultimately turned out to be several three to four inch squares of warm chocolate cake he had either just bribed for or swiped from the galley. As he began passing them around to his fellow quartermasters, beginning with his best friend first, he said with a laugh, "Hey, Sully, how's your tennis?"

"It ain't my racket!" came back Sullivan.

"OK, buddy, how's your golf?" Mickey further inquired, while passing the cake around.

"Today, I'm all teed-off at golf!" Sullivan answered, taking a bite of his cake.

"Something must be down your alley. What is it!"

"Bowling!" shouted Sullivan, his obvious answer ending the corny old vaudeville routine. And everybody laughed, mostly at their tone and actions. Toland had heard them greet each other with it at least once a day since they arrived back in port, and it sounded funny to him every time.

The chief accepted his slightly mashed piece of cake, took a bite, and then said to his leading quartermaster, "Let's knock off for the day, Brock. We're moving along OK, and I think we're gonna be up to date by the first of the year. What do you say?"

Brock answered in the affirmative and commented on the good efforts made by Harris, Sullivan, and Pollard in the last two weeks.

Toland smiled, took another bite of his cake, nodded to Mickey Harris, then left the wheelhouse. He heard Brock behind him clap his hands and order the stacks of charts picked up and the cleaning gear restowed.

The children were respectfully quiet as Verna's father, sitting at the head of the full table, offered a few short but sincere words of blessing and thanksgiving over the well-prepared dinner. Then everyone seemed to have something to say at the same time while passing and reaching for this bowl or that dish. Mace busied himself by carving the turkey. A few times during the course of the meal Toland's eyes met with Verna's, as was noticed by her father.

With the pumpkin pie almost gone and the adults turning down more coffee, Toland wanted to bring out his pipe for a smoke, but gave up on the idea for later. Then he observed Mr. Walker leave the table, with a slight show of effort, then return with a can of tobacco and his own curved stem pipe.

The children were anxious to leave the table to go out and play catch with the football, as Mace had promised they could earlier. The two women got up and began removing the dishes, over half of which ended back in Doris' kitchen. Whether they planned it or not, Toland was left alone with Mr. Walker, to become better acquainted. The last words heard over his shoulder were being spoken by Doris to her Charlie about the rudeness of the checkers and attendants she had to endure while getting her selection of food from the Navy Commissary the day before.

With his pipe in hand, Toland reached for his own tobacco, then accepted the middle-aged gentleman's offer to share some from his open can.

As Toland lit the clean-tasting tobacco, Walker got up again and selected a few records for his Victrola, asking over his shoulder if his guest liked good music. Toland didn't reply. Instead, he looked around the small living room. It was much the same as his friend's next door except it was obvious not as many children lived in this house. A reproduced painting of Christ in a kneeling position hung on one wall, while the opposite wall housed several dozen books in an inexpensive wooden case, perhaps built by Walker himself. And in the corner of the room nearest Toland a red and black checker board with a wooden box too big for just checkers rested on top of an old Philco radio.

"Boston Symphony!" he said proudly, and a slightly gritty recording of Chopin's Polonaise began to fill the room. Sitting back down, he was about to add another remark relating to the music when he noticed Toland glancing at his board and box.

"Do you play chess?" he asked with a smile.

"Yes, sir, once in awhile."

"Fine!" he answered. "That's fine. I only picked up the game a few months ago, myself. A friend taught me while I was in the hospital. I wish I had become better acquainted with it years ago. Such a marvelous game. Perhaps we'll try it later today." Then he added, "I've been hearing a lot about you this past week. And the boy likes you. Verna tells me you are in the navigation department of your ship. That's very interesting. I always thought of quartermasters as driving trucks and handling stores and things."

"No sir, that's in the Army," replied Toland, automatically.

It was obvious that Walker was trying to get an even conversation out of his guest and not meeting with much success. Then, looking at the table, he offered a more sincere and serious comment.

"I'm so sorry the world seems to be shaping up for another great war. I hope and pray we can stay out and avoid it this time. But then I am reminded by Mr. Hemingway over there," and he pointed to his books, "that this world is round, that we are all involved and part of the main, and what hurts one of us hurts us all. The bell tolls for each of us."

"Maybe that's true," answered Toland.

"Yes, of course. But you know what I think? I think someday the young people of this world are going to rise up and say 'stop it.' Because they're mostly the ones that have to get into the blood up to their necks. I think it will be a big movement someday, big as the Reformation. But it will have to be worldwide, you know?"

"Yes, sir."

Then he sighed again, and said, "But war seems such a romantic thing to them now. When it becomes a bore is when they'll rise up. Maybe it will happen next year."

"Maybe so," answered Toland.

The gentleman cast a long moment's stare in Toland's eyes, then smiled, "Meanwhile, our country wants to stay strong so that we can develop our noble, or petty, ideas, and someone always has to pay the price for them. I am glad I have no sons at this time."

He continued expounding on his personal views a while longer, then said, "Let's try that game of chess," and added modestly, "I'm very much a beginner you know!"

Over the years Toland had listened to a number of antimilitary or antiwar conversationalists. Some of whom had claimed a conscientious objection of one sort or another. Often it seemed to him it was their own conscience they were objecting to. Once, he even had a young man in his drafting office back in San Francisco a few months earlier angrily declare, "I know what you sailors do down in the bars of Hong Kong. I've heard and read all about you." Toland had shrugged it off, realizing the young man more probably was wishing he could have had a piece of the action for himself in the bars of Hong Kong or in any other place outside his own small existence. But this gentleman now in front of him was one of the few that had made comments of an objectionable nature that didn't smell of vanity or the sound of hatred for this or that political party or group of people. It was at least refreshing, and he could not help but like this short, paunchy man sitting across from him.

Halfway through the game, Verna came in and poured two fresh cups of coffee for her father and Toland. She wound up the Victrola again, placed the needle back down at the beginning, gave a nice smile to Toland, then left.

After she had departed, Walker leaned back from the game, at which he was doing well, and said, "I know my daughter is not beautiful, but she has a beautiful heart. And I think I should tell you this. She gives the impression that her husband died or was killed," he shook his head, then said, "He just up and left her and the boy some years ago. And she quietly got the divorce just last year." The chief listened and continued playing the game.

Late that afternoon Toland strolled with Verna down to the end of the street where the flooding had taken place the week before, and on the way back they made a date for the next evening.

They were both right on time as Toland spotted the little black coupé just on the other side of the Main Gate at 6 P.M. With the car in idle, Verna waved and slid over to the passenger side, allowing Toland to come around and take the wheel.

At a small, palm-infested, indoor-outdoor café on the west end of Waikiki Beach, they enjoyed a nice fish dinner together and later danced to requested American songs being played by four Hawaiian musicians from the high bandstand. A real tourist dive, Toland thought to himself, but as the evening wore on he found he was enjoying every minute of it. The only song he himself requested during the evening was 'Sophisticated Lady,' and they did it very well. It was not as good as Duke Ellington, but still pretty good. But the song most asked for from the growing group around them was 'I Don't Want to Set the World on Fire'! And by the third time the band had played it everyone, whether at their small tables or on the floor dancing, joined in and sang it.

Their first date together wasn't a body clincher, but they did have fun and enjoyed each other's company and found they had a number of things in common. It was the beginning of almost ten straight days of evenings and afternoons together. The only thing he didn't like about it was their goodnights at the Main Gate. It seemed to him he should be taking her home instead.

The following Wednesday, just before he left the ship, Toland received a package at mail call—a pair of tan leather house slippers with rubber soles, and a Christmas card inside signed by his two children. He was glad he had mailed them a few gifts earlier in the week. They had mailed their gift to him with the same idea in mind, of getting it to him before Christmas. The service had been good. It was the first word he'd had from them, although he had gotten two postal money orders off to his former wife since being aboard *Nevada*. The normal allotment wouldn't begin until January.

On Friday, Toland picked out a nice tortoise-shell hairpin at the Navy Exchange for Verna. At first he meant it as a Christmas gift but then couldn't resist giving it to her that night. It thoroughly delighted her, and she immediately placed it in her smooth long brown hair which was always rolled up in a bun either at the back or on the top of her head.

Although both were aware of each other's former marriage, the subject never came up in their conversations, which, for the most part, stayed light and uncomplicated. However, on Sunday afternoon, and while visiting the zoo located out near the east end of Waikiki Beach, a minor disagreement of sorts that could have developed into a major one came up. It began with a kidding remark from Toland about how much one of the monkeys behind the cage reminded him of a chief he knew back on his ship, and in a moment they were talking about evolution, reincarnation, and the like. Toland never had much faith in any specific Christian denomination. Moreover, he had concluded years earlier that they all had their petty flaws and overdone piety and they always seemed to build their strength on some interpretation completely disconnected from Matthew, Mark, Luke, and John. And though he didn't know quite how to put it into words, he realized that the animal in man including Christian man, could be more cruel and destructive than the wildest beasts living in the darkest jungles.

As they walked along discussing God, Christ, and evolution, Verna suddenly realized they might not have been talking on the same level. It was not that his views on the subject were more plausible than hers or that hers were more correct than his, but their level of thoughts were just different, possibly because their experiences were different. While passing the fenced-in ostrich area, she saw an opportunity of bringing things back in tune again by declaring, "Earl! You see that bird or animal or whatever it is over there? Well I've got this Aunt Evelyn back in—"

Toland looked down in her small face. He slowly smiled, then quickly realized what she was doing, and thought who the hell was he to debate the spiritual existence of man one way or another. He didn't know that much about it, anyway. They both looked at the huge bird that was now looking back at them; they grinned then laughed at each other and walked on.

Later that evening, Toland reminded her *Nevada* would get underway the next day for sea trials and then rejoin the Fleet if all went well, but would be back in port the following Friday, December 5, and that in all probability from here on *Nevada* would be spending her days at sea, then in port on the weekends, unless something unexpected came up. She promised to be waiting and expressed the hope that the past two weeks had been as nice for him as they had been for her. They had.

During the preceding week the relatively new and sleek light cruiser *Helena* moved in and tied up to Ten-Ten Dock just astern of *Nevada*. And now on this early Monday morning, beginning the first day of December, a half dozen or so of *Helena*'s deck hands were sent off and forward to assist the other handlers in casting off *Nevada*'s lines from the dock.

The wheelhouse teamwork seemed to Toland to move smoother than it had four weeks earlier when he first got underway with his new ship. A 'Ship of the Line,' the battleship was sometimes called, an expression carried over from the days of Sail and Nelson. And most every ship had its own nickname. The 'Cheer-Up-Ship'—that was *Nevada*'s! The reason for it? Everybody seemed to have his own idea as to how it come about. But she'd had it long before Honolulu, before Long Beach, and San Pedro. She always seemed to be in the right place at the right time and doing the right things, and she had a reputation of being a bit more of a happy ship than her sisters. Now the engine casualty was believed solved, and she was moving out to make sure. The captain himself had the conn this time. They were closer to the dredging vessel. More turns and quicker maneuvering would be required to negotiate Hospital Point, and they were much nearer to the mouth of the harbor than before. But equally important it was desirable that Flagship *Pennsylvania*, still in dry dock and scheduled to remain there at least two more weeks, should be a witness to *Nevada*'s good ship handling. Toland was beginning to feel some ownership and pride in her.

So it was with some anger and disappointment that the chief received the news again from Mickey Harris, in an almost identical manner as before, that another theft had taken place in the Operations living compartment. Only this time the article discovered missing was money, removed from a wallet belonging to one Thomas Hardy, Signalman Third Class. The wallet, declared by Hardy to have contained fourteen dollars, was back in the folds of his hammock minus the Christmas money he claimed to have been saving. The loss was discovered upon his return from the showers. Shadd was beyond suspicion as he did not make quarters that morning, and was listed as AWOL.

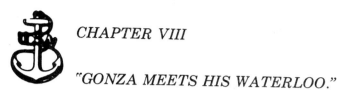

CHAPTER VIII

"GONZA MEETS HIS WATERLOO."

The slight drizzle that had been falling since early morning gave way to the stronger rays of sunlight as *Nevada* entered the open sea, with a steady on course of 180.

After securing from special sea detail, the captain waited another fifteen minutes, then gradually brought his ship up to flank speed at twenty-two knots, to commence sea trials. By 0930 the captain was more than satisfied with *Nevada*'s response and seaworthiness, and from Toland's DR ordered his ship into a swing to port and set a new course of 090, then slowed to standard speed, seventeen knots. The time of rendezvous with Battleship Divisions One and Two operating again off Maui was set at 1630 that evening, about the same as before. And as before, while in route, *Nevada* went through several exercises which included General Quarters. In each case the familiar term, "This is a drill, this is a drill," was piped throughout the ship. Battle readiness was set and clocked just under eight minutes. The captain was visibly pleased.

In the chilly mid-afternoon and just before securing from General Quarters, Toland's eyes fell on Morgan's gaze from across the wheelhouse. There was not the slightest hint of ease or friendship in the officer's stare. In a moment when he saw that Toland was alone and not so busy he approached the chief at the chart table. Leaning over the table and pushing his helmet slightly back, he said quietly, "Word has come to me there's been another theft. This time more than any two-bit camera." Still without looking directly at Toland he continued speaking to his chief quartermaster.

"I want you to get Hardy's dough back to him, and stop these thefts. Do you understand?"

Toland clinched his jaw and said, "Have you spoken to—"

"I'm not speaking to anyone else but you," he interrupted. And now, looking directly at Toland with a half smile, he said, "And I don't care how you do it. Just get it done. I'll back you up if you need it, and I might break you if you don't get it done. Do you understand now, Chief?"

Toland remained rigid and did not answer as he stared back at his operations officer.

Morgan raised up from the table just as the captain, happy with the results of GQ, ordered the bosun to announce secure, and a return to the regular underway steaming watch.

Sitting across the mess table from Gonza, Toland knew he had the winning cards. Stuckey to his right had folded, as did Pops sitting at the end of the table at Toland's left. And now the chief carpenter at Gonza's left turned over his cards. Gonza, wearing a broad grin, raised the bet again. It was just Toland and Gonza now. But the chief signalman had to be bluffing in their game of five-card stud. He had two pair showing, queens and fours, while Toland had three nines and a deuce up. All the cards had been dealt, and they each had one card down. Toland's fourth nine had been turned over with the carpenter's hand, as they both knew, and the other twos were scattered between Stuckey and Pops, and this was one reason they turned over early. As for Gonza's other queens and fours, they too were all accounted for, except for one queen. It could have been Gonza's bottom card which would have filled him up, but it wasn't. Toland held the queen of spades as his own down card. Gonza had to be bluffing.

But this wasn't altogether what Toland had on his mind as he glanced at the clock over Gonza's left shoulder. Any minute now, two more at the most, the action would begin. And the action would have little or nothing to do with the cards in front of them. It was now Thursday evening, December 4, and it was their fourth day at sea. *Nevada* would secure from the week's exercises on the following morning, take her place in formation, and head back for another weekend in Pearl with the rest of the Fleet.

On Monday, after Morgan's demand that he straighten out the Division's problems of money and theft, Toland had done nothing about it that day. He did, however, think that perhaps he should have tried something earlier against Gonza's slush fund that seemed to be putting a hardship and drain on the Division's personnel and their resources. But now he must, he decided, do something. So Tuesday afternoon he started a quiet investigation of his own. Toland found that Hardy also was into the fund some thirty dollars, and by Wednesday afternoon had discovered that over half the division was tied to it in various amounts, some individuals being as much as seventy-five dollars in arrears. And there were others outside the Division who were also in 'debt' to Gonza.

Toland thought of various ways he could stop it; any number of them would have worked. After all it was strictly against Naval Regulations to become involved in any moneylending operation aboard ship. But to stop it in such a way that it wouldn't start up again later, and also to stop it without a 'mast' or court-martial which might involve a number of other people—that was going to be the trick. On this Thursday afternoon, and after securing from the exercises and drills of the day, and as *Nevada* made for her usual night-steam area, Gonza himself provided and invited the way.

"How 'bout it, Wheels, you want in?"

"Too close to payday, old buddy. Maybe next time," Toland answered the chief signalman, as he was about to return to his charts on the bridge.

Gonza, sitting down at the mess table, now with a green felt blanket over one end, smiled at his consenting poker players then looked at Toland again, and said, "How much do ya need? I'll spot ya. We want a fifth player anyway." Then Gonza began placing a stack of bills and some change in front of himself.

Toland hesitated, then quickly realized his opportunity. He said, "A hundred!"

Gonza made a long low whistle, then laughed, "A full yard! The man's out for our blood. OK, buddy-boy, but I got a rule. You pay back tonight, or tomorrow it's interest. A deal?"

"A deal!" Toland answered, "You get these bills back tonight, or it's interest tomorrow."

Toland wanted to say, maybe I am out for your blood, Gonza buddy, but he held it.

Gonza pushed four twenties and two tens in Toland's direction. The chief quartermaster shoved the bills in his pocket without counting them and said he would be back shortly, after checking the 'night orders' on the bridge. Gonza made a motion for him to leave the bills on the table, then made a 'to-hell-with-it' look as he began to buy himself a stack of chips that were being counted out by Stuckey.

"Count me out twenty bucks' worth to start. I'll be back in a minute," declared Toland.

Within minutes after reaching his charthouse, Toland had Harris, Sullivan, and Hardy making change and counting out the bills into their somewhat reluctant hands. One of Gonza's crisp ten dollar bills was left over.

"OK, Mick. That should do it. Now, let's get it straight again. You all go down together. You knock on the door at exactly 1930, an hour from now. You walk in, pay the man what you owe him. No questions asked and no smart remarks. And then you walk out. I'll take it from there. And if either of you ever get this ship or yourselves involved in a slush fund again, I'll personally write you up, myself." Toland felt that Mickey Harris would be the least likely one to show up in front of the chiefs' mess on time, so he said, "Mick, you make sure these guys show up on time, and with the dough in hand, OK?"

"Right, Chief, gotcha!"

Now Toland felt they would make it on time. Then he sent Sullivan up to relieve Brock for a few minutes, who now had the watch. In a moment Toland, still in the charthouse, was speaking privately to an eager Brock, who was listening with quiet delight.

"Then tomorrow morning after you hold reveille in the compartment you explain that all debts are hereby canceled, with Chief Gonza's gift for the holidays. And hereafter there will be no more slush funds; then you get ahold of Chief Gonza's collector, and in a friendly way relieve him of his record book and deep-six it. Now get back on watch."

"I can do it tonight, Chief."

"You'll wait until after reveille tomorrow!"

On his way out, Brock said, more to himself than to Toland, "Gonza finally meets his Waterloo."

Before reentering the chiefs' mess Toland folded Gonza's crisp ten that was left over, into a glider, and then smiled as he opened the door. Thirty had gone to Hardy. Sullivan had owed twenty-five, and Harris was in it for thirty-five.

From his wallet Toland removed a twenty of his own and purchased the chips in front of him, then sailed the folded ten into Gonza's stack, "Sorry, old buddy, but ninety was all I needed."

Although there remained fixed smiles on the two men's faces, it was obvious to the others at the table the enmity between them was growing fast.

Toland lost the first few hands. He dropped out early, waiting for a better one to come along, then in five-card stud dealt by Pops he hit three nines and a lone deuce to Gonza's queens and fours a pair. He called Gonza's bluffing raise, then without raising back turned over the queen of spades.

Gonza lost his smile for a moment then forced it back, and said, "Well, you can't win 'em all."

"That's right, ol' buddy," answered Toland as he began dragging in the healthy pot, "you can't win 'em all." And without looking up at the knock that came on the chiefs' door he began stacking his chips.

Sheepishly the three sailors came in with their hats off, and it was Mickey first that laid down his money in front of Gonza, and with a shaky smile said, "This squares us, Chief. You can check your books if you wanta."

Sullivan made a similar remark, followed by Hardy who only smiled as he laid the thirty in front of his chief. Before the three men departed, Gonza had counted the money, cast an irritating glance at them, and threw one menacing look at Toland, who was no longer smiling. He got the big picture.

The chief signalman arose from the table like a wounded bear, and if it hadn't been bolted to the deck it would have been knocked clean over, taking the chips with it. Toland, a half head shorter than Gonza, continued counting and stacking his winning chips, but his reflex was tight and ready for whatever might come. Toland may have been a number of things, but one thing he was not. He was not afraid of any one man alive. He figured his own ugly face had been bruised and cut before through the years, and a few more of them wouldn't make that much difference to him now. And anyway, he had always been able to hold his own or better. He would this time too if it came down to it.

On his feet, Stuckey was ready to intervene physically. He did intervene verbally. "You guys want to settle it with baseball bats ashore, that's OK with me. But not on this ship!"

Toland stood up and said to Stuckey while looking straight at Gonza's angry red face, "Check me out! Sixty-eight dollars and forty cents," then to the chief signalman, "There will be no more slush funds in Operations! Retire from the lending profession, buddy. You made enough by now."

"What about that 'yard' I just lent you," Gonza said, finding the ability to speak for the first time since standing up.

"You've got it in front of you. Check it!" replied Toland, and added, "What you haven't got anymore is the Division. Check that out with the Captain, on down to Ensign Lord if you want. You're retired from that, too. And my liberty section is posted, if you want to check with me later somewhere else."

"Now that sounds fair enough to me," said Pops, with a helpful grin, "let's get back to the game."

Toland bit the inside of his cheek then said, "Suits me, if we can keep it peaceful."

At 1600 on the following afternoon the mighty battlewagons of the proud Pacific Fleet began standing into Pearl for their final bit of weekend peace. Three of these would go to their deaths and enter the pages of history within forty-one hours. Destiny was near at hand now. But not for "Lady Lex." Not yet, anyway. The *Lexington* was one day out of Pearl headed for Midway to drop off a load of planes for that island's defense, should they be needed. But destiny would catch up to her too, soon enough. Five months to the day to be exact. And even the great Butch O'Hare wouldn't be able to save her from going to the bottom of the Coral Sea as he would do almost singlehandedly near Rabaul three months earlier. But now, both carriers were at sea and safe from harm's way, for the moment at least.

Nevada was about the last capital ship in the harbor to become moored to her assigned berth. One of several small

Navy tugs that had been scampering up and down the line of battleships like sheep-herding dogs, making sure their huge burdens were snug against their mooring buoys and posts along Ford Island's Battleship Row for the weekend, now turned its attention to *Nevada*, which already had one tug pushing against her port quarter. And on signal from the First Lieutenant the little gray tug took station on *Nevada*'s port bow, and she too assisted in nuzzling the mighty ship up against the northernmost mooring posts along the Row. Line handlers already on the pilings received the heavy thimble eyes and clamped them in place, while on *Nevada*'s gun decks, lines of seamen began taking in the slack.

"Moored! Shift colors!" the bosun commanded. There was still a little time before sunset, and *Nevada*'s in-port colors went up on the fantail as her smaller battle colors came down from the main.

A meeting in the officers' wardroom had been called away, and liberty was being delayed until further notice, pending a decision being discussed in the wardroom as to whether or not to continue operating on a five-section liberty basis. There was some talk in reducing it to three sections and keeping a larger amount of personnel on board. But the fact was that most men stayed aboard anyway except for the first few days after payday. And the next pay call was not until Monday, December 8. They would discuss it again, then.

The long motor launches were already in the water and lying off when the word was passed, "Now Liberty Call! Liberty will commence for Sections One, Three, Four, and Five at 1730. Liberty to expire on board for Section One at 0800 tomorrow morning."

Toland, in the red leather couch was ready and waiting, and put down the five-day-old paper as Mace stuck his head in the chiefs' mess to announce, "There's a boat alongside set to shove off. Let's make it, Earl!"

The headlines across the *Honolulu Advertiser* read,

"Japan Called Still Hopeful of Making Peace."

On the boat ride to Fleet Landing, and during part of the walk to the Main Gate Toland and Mace passed a few words between themselves regarding the rumors and scuttlebutt floating around mostly about the directives coming in from Washington advising all forces in the Pacific to go on an alert. A large body of Japanese troops that was being escorted by a sizable naval force near Formosa had been sighted some days ago by an American submarine on patrol in that area. The crypto rooms aboard heavy Naval vessels in Pearl were humming all right, but very few messages were sent directly to them. In some cases the Flags were made information-addressees, but that was about it. The big stuff from Washington was going directly to CINCPAC, and he'd know how to handle it.

But with the Main Gate near, and Doris almost in view—she had spotted her man now and was vigorously waving from the other side—Mace reminded his friend that he had the weekend duty and would have to be back on board the next morning. It was hardly worth going ashore for.

Toland sat in the rear seat as Doris drove back through town. Mace, sitting up front beside his wife, complained that he was in no mood to see a movie that night.

"Now, Charlie. Please do this one thing for me, and I won't ask another thing from you for a whole year. And that's a promise, OK, honey? Verna and me, we just want to see this show so bad. We're going to pick her up at Thomas Square and then we're all going right to dinner from there."

Then she explained that Verna's father was sort of babysitting with the children at his home, and Leon was in charge, and that they wanted to hear their radio programs with the lights turned off. "The Shadow," "Inner Sanctum," and a terrible one called "The Witches' Tails"!

Mace looked back at Toland and said, "Dammit, those

were exactly the ones I wanted to hear." Then he said to Doris, "Woman! Take us home!"

"I will do no such thing!" she replied, defiantly. And in a moment everyone laughed, and Mace reached over to kiss the side of her neck.

Verna's trim figure came into view almost as soon as the car completed the turn on to Kapiolani Street. And now in the back seat with Toland, she immediately began to explain what Doris had already passed on to him. She had had to work a little later than usual, as two people had gotten mixed up in their appointments for getting their teeth cleaned, and her car was parked in a good place near the cafeteria-style restaurant they had selected. Then she confessed she hadn't seen many movies in her lifetime, her denominational faith having always frowned upon such things, but this time Doris' descriptions had been too tempting.

At dinner Toland announced that he was picking up the tab for the entire evening.

"Let him do it!" Mace agreed, then he began elaborating on Toland's taking over the division and the apparent success he had in ending some of Operations' difficulties. He hadn't been there at the time but had heard all about it from Pops and Lacey.

Later that evening, when Tyrone Power began coming down the crowded gangway of the troop transport and with a bloody bandage around his head waving to—then falling in the waiting arms of—Betty Grable, Doris had to quietly blow her nose in her handkerchief. Verna was also visibly touched. *A Yank in the RAF*, playing at the Waikiki Theater, was thoroughly enjoyed by most everyone in the audience. Mace, however, had fallen asleep at the most touching moment.

Saturday, the next morning, Toland slept late on the couch while Doris fixed an early breakfast for her husband then drove him down in time to catch the 0750 liberty boat back to his ship. Toland awoke to find he was alone in the house and took advantage of the family's absence to shower and clean up in privacy.

By the time Doris returned, Toland had a pot of coffee almost made. She came in with Verna and two of the children who had crossed the wet lawn to meet her as she pulled into the driveway. Over the fresh coffee the women decided, if it was all right with Toland, they should all drive up to the Pali and observe the spot where King Kamehameha had foiled his enemies centuries ago—after they each got their houses cleaned up, of course.

The surrounding view of the island, with the green hills of Molokai coming up in the distance, made a breathtaking view as they trooped around Tantalus Peak. But it was all ignored as Verna, tired from the hike, relaxed back on a grassy knoll. She removed her tortoise-shell pin and let her hair fall down around her back and shoulders. It was the first time Toland had seen her without her hair all rolled up in a bun. After a few moments of playful actions and words, she asked the question, "Will you go to church with me next Saturday?"

"Saturday!" Toland answered. "What's wrong with Sunday?"

"Well, there's a very good reason."

"That I should go to church on Saturday, or that I should just go to church?" he answered, in a kidding manner while playing with a few strands of her hair. "And what's wrong with Thursday? Why does everybody leave out Tuesday and Thursday? What the hell did they do that was so wrong?"

Then Verna raised up on one elbow and attempted to explain her church's beliefs and philosophy, and spoke of the Great Disappointment.

"Look, honey," Toland broke in, "I just don't believe in all that hocus-pocus." Then he inadvertently gave her a ray of hope as he added, "Maybe it's all you Christians I don't believe in, going around hurting and killing each other, generation after generation."

She looked at him hard and long for a few moments, then started to confess she had had her own doubts and that she and her father had not been as devout members of their church as they might have wished, but that her faith in God and Christ and people in general was unshakable.

But just then Doris came over, a bit tousled, and made her confession that she was exhausted from trying to handle three wild indians. But she was careful not to unduly disturb the little romance she felt she had begun.

It was three in the afternoon when they reached home again, and Toland, acknowledging Verna's comment of her father's enjoyment of the game, agreed to offer him a challenge to another game of chess. Anyway, the women wanted to discuss some private things.

At 3:46 a child's scream came from the yard outside, and a moment or two later Verna came in exclaiming Cathy had hurt her arm, maybe had broken it. They had been playing with the football, and Donald had tackled her on the grass or something. Toland quickly left the table and Mr. Walker for the house next door, and after examining her arm Toland realized it was wrenched pretty bad. Cathy continued crying for her father. In a few more moments it was all decided what to do. Verna would drive Doris and Cathy to the emergency hospital located inside the Sea Plane Base at Kaneohe, while Toland would take the Studebaker back to the main gate parking lot, board the first liberty boat back to *Nevada*, and, with permission from the CDO, stand by for Mace. Mace should be back at Kaneohe by 5:00, 5:30 at the most, depending on how often the boats were running. Doris, with a long Navy wife's understanding, said Mace would not want Toland to stand by for him any longer than would be necessary and that he would probably be back sometime Sunday morning.

"Thanks, buddy," Mace said, while putting on a clean white uniform and getting the news and a brief rundown on the situation from Toland. "She's probably just busted it or something. She broke her other arm two years ago. What a tomboy! I wish she'd start playing with dolls for a change." Reaching over and quietly closing his locker door, he added, "I'll be back around colors tomorrow morning."

Toland told him to stay the weekend if he wanted, but knew his friend meant what he said. He would be back on board Sunday morning.

CHAPTER IX

"WE ARE BEING SHOT AT! THIS AIN'T NO DRILL!"

"Jack-of-the-Dust" was passed by the bosun on the early morning watch. The pleasant smell of fresh-made bread drifted through the passageways as other bakers and duty cooks and mess cooks were being rousted to prepare Sunday morning's breakfast. For more than fifty of *Nevada's* crew it would be their last. And of the surviving nine hundred or so, of which many would be permanently maimed and wounded, they would thrill or bore people about this day for the rest of their lives.

Toland pulled his left arm from under his pillow, studied the luminous dial at his wrist, then reached for his pipe from the beam ledge above his head. It was 0545. A mild chorus of snoring swelled up from the few duty chiefs still soundly sleeping around him.

He had had a restless night, and for no reason awoke twice during the early hours. He thought of Verna and figured it must have been because of their disagreement and near-argument the afternoon before.

No more of that kind of stuff, he thought, we'll iron it out OK, and decided to call her before noon. He also decided he not only loved her, he liked her, and was just about sure she felt the same for him.

As he sat on the edge of his bunk he recalled how she always smoothed her skirt down before sitting. When she spoke there seemed to be an absence of confidence in her own opinions, but had the courage to speak them, while her forefinger would unconsciously push back the cuticle of her left thumb. And he thought of her crooked lower teeth and apparent years of habit of not smiling broadly, fearing they would show too much. And if he told her a story she found exceptionally funny, her large brown eyes would seem to grow even larger, but her hands would always reach her mouth just before laughing.

"We'll have a two-person luau down near Kualoa Point this very afternoon," he told himself. "She likes picnics and will really go for that idea!" And he redecided to call her, right after colors. Mace would be back aboard by then.

On his way to the head Toland lit the stale tobacco still left in his pipe. After two puffs he looked at it in disgust, then knocked the ashes out in the toilet bowl.

He was right in the middle of a brisk shower, soaped down and scrubbing away, when the steady hum of the ship's generators began to slow down. The lights in the head faded, as he looked up at the trickling nozzle. It wouldn't be the first time Toland would be caught in the shower with a power failure. But it was only momentary, and things were humming again, lights bright as ever, maybe even a little brighter. The chief let out a sigh of relief, and he too was humming and scrubbing away again.

After brushing his teeth, a careful shave and following up with a liberal amount of lotion all sailors refer to as 'foo-foo juice,' he got into a clean set of underwear and put on fresh-starched khaki shirt and trousers. And, as usual, he gave a few moments' thought to his children Stateside while putting on his comfortable house slippers instead of his brown shoes.

On Sundays the bugler doesn't blow his horn, but the word is still passed, "Reveille, reveille! Sweepers, man your brooms. Give the ship a clean sweep down, fore and aft. Breakfast for the crew!"

With his cloth cap on Toland climbed the ladder to the main deck and met one of the CPO mess cooks at the top.

Sleepy-eyed, the boy managed a smile and suggested a cup of hot coffee for the chief.

"Let's you and me have one together, OK?" Toland said, putting his hand on the young man's shoulder and adding, "You get the coffee going and I'll get a Sunday paper off the Quarterdeck." Toland was aware he was just beginning his sixth week aboard *Nevada*.

Grinning and more awake now the young sailor answered, "Ok, Chief. You like your eggs scrambled, right?"

"Right, buddy!"

Toland stepped from the aft main deck hatch into the warm golden sunshine. Ensign Toby had the deck, and the chief saluted him as he approached. Each man genuinely liked each other but maintained a strictly military association. Toby was a good example of Annapolis training and the kind of officer men respect.

Smiling and returning the salute, he said, "Good morning, Chief. I didn't know you had the duty!"

"Good morning, Mr. Toby. I'm just standing by for Chief Mace until Colors. He had the duty weekend but had a little difficulty at home. He should be back aboard with the second liberty boat." Toland glanced at his watch. It was 0655.

"The first one's coming out now," Toby said, then over his shoulder, "Bosun, pass the word for the relieving boat crew to man their stations."

For a few moments Toby and the chief watched the approaching motor launch together. Not even a pelican disturbed the serene peace and tranquillity of the ninety-five other American Naval vessels moored or anchored around them. Pearl Harbor's clear green water was slick as a mirror except that part which was being almost rudely disturbed by *Nevada*'s returning boat. Two long, ever widening streams turning to ripples followed behind in a V shape, one end pointing to the sub base and the other to the shipyard and Ten-Ten Dock. The top of the white foam being pushed up by the bow of the oncoming boat gave the appearance of shimmering gold and silver coins scattering before it. And in the wet haze made by the boat's movement a distinct portion of a rainbow appeared.

Toby looked up at the few fluffs of white clouds moving eastward, then at the green hillsides around him, and said, "Beautiful morning, eh, Chief?" He almost said, 'Glorious morning.'

From their viewpoint neither man could see the nets parting at the mouth of the harbor, allowing a small American Naval vessel to stand in. And even if they could, it would only have been a routine observation anyway.

"It sure is," Toland truthfully replied. Then glancing around, he added, "Let's hope it stays that way!" He was hoping for a day without rain.

"If you're looking for the Sunday paper you'll find a copy in the Chiefs' Mess. The water taxi came by an hour ago. Incidentally, Church Call will go down at 0900, and Chaplin Donahue always has a good sermon. Hope to see you then."

"Yes, sir. I'll think about it," said Toland. Then before turning away he asked about the temporary loss of power which had occurred during his shower.

Toby stated that number one boiler and generator had been carrying the load all weekend, and he decided to light off and cut in number two to take off the strain. A decision, together with his other acts of wisdom and courage this day, would move him up the ladder of his professional Naval career sooner than he ever expected.

On his way back down to the chiefs' mess, Toland found the passageways a little more active now, and passed two bandsmen with their instruments heading for the fantail. They were arguing about who won the battle of the ships' jazz bands that was staged the night before to a packed crowd of encouraging sailors at Block Arena. One was stubborn in his opinion that the *Arizona* had won it, the other defending the final decision of the judges with, "Man, the *Pennsylvania* won it hands down!"

They allowed the chief a moment's greeting, then continued their argument on up the ladder. It was the practice of *Nevada*'s band to play The Star Spangled Banner each Sunday morning on the fantail at Colors, in port, when possible, weather permitting, and when enough of them were available. These conditions were all met on this Sunday morning, December 7, 1941.

The black and white Seth-Thomas clock fastened to the mahogany paneling in the chiefs' lounge, ticked away at 0718 when Mace stepped inside.

"Earl, boy, what you eating? Smells good, and I'm hungry as a Marine Staff Sergeant!"

"I thought you weren't coming back until the second boat," Toland said, putting down his paper and pushing back from the table.

The mess cook smiled and greeted Mace while clearing away the empty breakfast dishes in front of Toland.

"The works, buddy, with four over easy," he said over his shoulder, while hanging up his white coat and loosening his tie.

"Right away, Chief!" the young man called back.

"Guess who was on the boat with me—His 'Lordship'! He stayed on his side and I stayed on mine. But," Mace continued, throwing one arm in the air, "I'll hear from him before the morning's out." Then, pouring his black coffee from the stainless steel urn, "I saw Verna before I left the house this morning," and turned around to catch Toland's expression.

"OK, what did she say?"

"I didn't say she said anything, I just said I saw her!" he said, smiling.

Toland cocked his head a little and patiently waited.

"OK, OK, I was just kidding," said Mace, as he sat down with his coffee across from his friend. "She caught me as I was driving out in the old jalopy. She said you should call her. Something about a picnic this afternoon. Just you and her, she said." Then taking a sip, "She really likes you, Earl. I can't imagine why," he said curtly, then adding warmly, "but she really does like you."

"I was thinking about calling her sometime today," Toland half lied. Then smiling, "I think I'll call her right after colors."

"Listen, you can take the 'Studie' back this morning. Doris is going to have to do some shopping this afternoon, anyway. I left the keys under the seat."

Changing the subject, Toland asked, "How's your kid? How's Cathy?"

"She's OK. Did you know a sprained arm can hurt you worse than a broken arm, did you know that? Anyway she's home from the hospital and is going to stay indoors the next couple of days. You know what she was worried about the most?" he said, gulping down some of his coffee. "She was worried she would have to wear that cast over Christmas. Ain't that typical of kids? Can't interfere with Christmas, you know."

The mess cook put four eggs and a large slice of ham in front of Mace and, without being asked, brought over a fresh cup of coffee for Toland, who was glancing at the clock over the right of Mace's head. It moved on, passing 0732.

"Glad to hear she's OK. I'll bet Donald feels bad about it right now. He's a good kid."

"You're not kidding, Earl. Why, that boy was waiting on our door step till ten last night when we brought Cathy back home. And you know what? Cathy kissed him on the cheek, and told him it didn't hurt a bit. Now that's the first time I ever saw her kiss anyone outside the family. Yep, she's really growing up. You should have some kids of—" Mace stopped chewing and looked apologetically at Toland, then continued eating.

"Now, relieve the watch. The Eight-to-Twelve watch, relieve the watch!" It was 0745.

Toland went back to reading his Sunday paper from the

place he left off when his friend came in. In a few minutes, he said, "Things don't look so good, Mace. I think we're going to have to get in the ring with them pretty soon." Then he added with a blank stare at the edge of the table, "And I don't like the way the Fleet just hangs in Pearl like this."

"Well, Hitler's subs are a long way from here. The way I see it—"

"No, buddy. I'm talking about Japan."

"Yeah, I know what you mean. Them damn Japs, I don't trust any of them, not even a little bit. Here they are pushin' away in China, grabbin' up ground in French Indo, and all the time they got 'peacemakers' in Washington."

"First call, first call to Colors!" The word was passed over the squawk box, at exactly 0755.

"Say, buddy!" Toland asked, "Just why did you take the first liberty boat back instead of the second?"

"Well, after last night Doris didn't feel so good, so this morning—" the big ship moved a little and the coffee still in their cups quivered at the surface.

"Well, Doris didn't feel so good—" he began again, both men looking straight at each other as the ship swayed around them, something like the feel of the first groundswell when putting out to sea. Only they were not putting out to sea.

"Earl?" Mace said to Toland who was clinching his jaw and looking down at his coffee in front of him.

The PA system clicked on again but no voice came right away, but clearly the sound of an airplane came through, then faded. Some shouting around the PA mike, then a shaky but determined voice said, "All hand, all hands, man your battle stations!"

Both men's faces were now glued to the box in the corner. Mace's features were contorted, but he managed part of a smile as he said, "GQ drills on Sunday? Now that's carrying things too—" He was interrupted again as

136

both men and the disturbed mess cook heard a noise something like one might hear when striking a pillow to fluff it up, then *Nevada* really lurched to port. "—far! I've got to get to my radio shack!" All three men made a dash for the door without taking anything with them. Toland was nearer and got through first, and into the swift traffic of startled men running in both directions.

Once more the PA system spoke, only this time with a different, more determined voice. "This is no drill, get off your damn butts and man your battle stations! We are being shot at, this ain't no drill!!"

The passageways would have been even more confused and crowded were it not true that most of *Nevada*'s men were still in the sack. Mace was right behind Toland, up the ladder, through the mess decks and all the way up to the 04 level to his radio room opposite the captain's sea cabin, and there they parted, forever.

But even before getting to the 02 level the smell of gunpowder was in their nostrils. Shouting voices up ahead mixed in with the whine of aircraft engines and the unlikely sound of bomb bursts. Even so, Toland more than halfway expected to see the same peaceful Pearl Harbor scene he and Ensign Toby shared together hardly an hour earlier. He even thought he heard band music somewhere far behind him.

What greeted the chief, instead, as he reached the wheelhouse deck, was a roaring head-on approach of a greenish-looking airplane. It had just dropped something, and with wings spurting fire came screaming on in.

Toland dove, hit, then slid across the deck into a pile of helmets rolling around near the open helmet locker. He didn't waste time getting one on. Glass and paint were breaking up all around inside the wheelhouse. Lying against the port bulkhead, the chief caught glimpses through the window, and then the open hatch, of the same plane banking off on the starboard side of his ship. Clearly he saw a painted red ball under each wing. "Japs!" Toland said aloud, then louder almost quizzically, "Goddamn Japs!" Then he felt the whomp of the torpedo slam into his ship somewhere far below.

"DC Central, report!" he heard someone hollering from outside the open port hatch.

Toland felt himself begin to shake. He was scared. That was a blessing. He knew he was scared. He gripped the side of the locker next to him and hollered loud as he could, "Dammit, dammit. Dammit!" then he didn't seem to be shaking anymore.

"Is that you, Chief Toland? Are you all right?" came the voice of Lieutenant Commander Morgan.

"Yes, sir, I'm fine. How about yourself!"

"I'm OK. Glad you're here. The skipper and XO, and most of the officers are ashore, but most of the crew's aboard." They were looking at each other and talking from either side of the open port hatch. Morgan with his head set on and a recorder kneeling beside him were crouched down as low as Toland, then he began talking into his phones again, "Don't clog the circuit, speak slowly and distinctly, not on top of each other, just cool down! Now report! And give me that signal again. —No, that's impossible right now".

Toland got to his feet, and with knees still bent got his first full panoramic view of the strange holocaust going on in the harbor and on the other ships around him. No, it wasn't the same.

A fire, and heavy black smoke was billowing up over near Hickam Field. A half dozen planes or so were coming in on a nice clean pattern from over the shipyard, streams of gray smoke following behind most of them, and heading for the battleships moored ahead of *Nevada*. As they skimmed low toward their targets, torpedoes would drop, splash, and continue on their course as the planes reached for altitude again. Toland counted five torpedo wakes at one time. Geysers shooting skyward followed in succession, then explosion sounds a second or two later. Pearl Harbor was churning now with torpedo wakes and several half-full liberty boats with men trying to get back to their ships. Some ship's guns, almost surprisingly, began shooting back.

"Hey, Chief!" the voice of Jimmy Pollard called out, "Ain't this something?"

Toland left the nearly unbelievable view and hurried over to the starboard wing and crouched down with the figure outside. "Well, Jimmy, you hit the nail squarely on the head. Now, have you got anybody else on those phones?"

"Yeah, Mickey is on the port wing same as me—yeah, Mick, the Chief's here!" he spoke into his mouth piece. Then looking back at Toland, "All the guys are aboard. Sully ought to be coming up with Brock pretty soon. They were both in their sacks when the Mick and me came up to help with Prep and Colors. Honest, Chief, I got to tell you this. I never was sure the Japs were coming. I just guessed it, honest!"

"It was a good guess, Jimmy. A few other people around here should have guessed as well, I think. Now, what signalmen are on the bridge?"

"Hardy, Slaughter, and one other guy, Milton, I think," he answered thoughtfully.

"I'm going to get my phones on and we'll have a three-way fix, OK? Now just sit tight!"

"OK, Chief. And you know," he added, "you're the best chief we ever had."

Toland was about to answer but changed his mind, winked at Jimmy instead, then stepped back inside. He got his phones from under the chart table, removed his helmet and quickly harnessed himself in, then pressed down on the little button and said, "Navigation checking in, how do you read me!"

"Five by five!" Jimmy answered.

"Loud and clear!" came Mickey's voice. Then he said, "We thought you were on liberty, Chief. Sure glad you weren't!"

"That's a matter of opinion we'll discuss later, but right now I want you both to keep alert, but keep alive too. I want you to stand up just far enough to keep a good clear view of what's going on around you and on your side. When you see a plane heading our way, report it, then get the hell down where you are, or jump inside here whatever you think best at the time. Have you got that?"

"Yeah, Chief!" said Jimmy.

"Gotcha!" answered Mickey's voice. "Boy, this is better than the movies. I'm sure glad I'm in the Navy."

Toland almost ordered them to knock off the chatter but thought their spirits would stay higher if they could keep talking a little.

The short reprieve in the attack on *Nevada* ended abruptly when Mickey called out, not one but several aircraft coming *Nevada*'s way.

"OK, Mick, now get down flat on your belly!" Toland couldn't tell whether he heard him or not the roar was so great. The bulkheads and decks shook as *Nevada*'s antiaircraft batteries began to answer.

Through the shock and the yellow fumes filling up the wheelhouse, Toland caught a glimpse of Walter Sullivan, inching his way in through the open port hatch. The chief reached for one of the helmets rolling around next to him and threw it over to the large teenage boy crawling toward him, then motioned to him to stop where he was and stay down. He got the helmet all right but kept coming toward Toland.

Then the noise died down somewhat, and a cheer went up out on the port side. Mickey's voice came in loud and clear, "We got one of them—maybe two of them!"

Toland smiled and held up two fingers to Sullivan, who didn't smile back. Now, sitting up next to his chief on the deck, Sullivan said, "Sorry I'm late getting up here." Then

140

he wiped the sweat from his forehead with his shirt sleeve.
"That's OK, Sully, we're all a little late. Where's Brock!"

Crawling through the port hatch with his phones hanging about his head, Mickey said to his best friend, "Hey, Sully, you bastard! Where ya been? You missed the whole show!"

"The show's not over yet, sailor. Now get back out there and keep a good watch," Toland answered.

"But you said we could—"

"I know what I said. Now get back out there!" After Mickey passed back onto the port wing, Toland turned to Sullivan again, "Where's Brock?"

"He just didn't make it, Chief! We were coming up together—he was in front of me. We were coming up on the port side weather ladder, we're supposed to come up on the port side, you know? Well," he caught his breath, "a blast came, and he just wasn't there any more. I think he blew over the side."

"OK, OK, that's enough. Just don't mention it right now, OK?" Toland slapped him gently on his cheek. "Now get me Pearl's tide and current data for today. Get to it, Sailor! Get the book and get over in the corner there."

Toland put him to work mostly to get his mind busy, then turned from Sullivan back to the continuing disaster around him. He thought *Nevada* seemed low at the bow and leaning to port. The pitch and yaw arms still in place on the overhead confirmed it. A degree and a half on each. There were no more torpedo planes, but Toland didn't trust the present lull in the attack.

Then it came, as the chief watched *Vestal* pull away from *Arizona*, which was tied to the buoys dead ahead. Bombs from high-level planes began screaming down, splash and straddle *Nevada* and the other dreadnoughts moored along Ford Island's Battleship Row.

Toland pressed down on his button and said, "Everybody inside! Come on in, right now! Mickey, holler up to the signal bridge. Get them down here if you can."

Morgan had the same idea and came in with his recorder and removed one receiver from his left ear. He was haggard and looked five years older. "I called up to the signal bridge but got no answer. God, did you see her go over, Chief?" Toland's expression said no, so Morgan continued, "God, *Oklahoma*! She started listing and kept on going, just kept on going. Right on over!"

Toland went to the wheelhouse window. Just then he saw bomb bursts moving along *Arizona's* decks. The relentless enemy planes high above were finding their mark. And then the one that would cost her more than a thousand lives struck her magazines. A huge, engulfing, bright yellow flash followed by a concussion that bent and warped *Nevada's* entire bridge wings and bulkheads with heat. Everyone in *Nevada's* wheelhouse was knocked down and nearly senseless. Most were sure it was *Nevada* coming apart. Although the explosion instantly killed a dozen of *Nevada's* men who were on or near the bow, it was *Arizona* that blew up and completely suffered the death blow. All that was left of her was a mass of twisted burning bulkheads and braces. Her back broken open, she immediately settled to the bottom, with just her twisted superstructure sticking out above the burning oily water in a grotesque, agonizing shape.

CHAPTER X

*"I'VE GOT AXES
ON IT NOW, CHIEF.—UNDERWAY!
WE'RE NOT ALL DEAD
DOWN HERE YET, SAILOR!"*

Every man in the wheelhouse was shocked and surprised to find he wasn't on his way to eternity, yet. Somehow, each of them came to his own personal reality that he was still alive, still in one piece, and *Nevada* was still very much around him and floating. Some just concluded it more quickly than others.

Every window left in the wheelhouse was cracked beyond vision; a few were blown completely out. Toland stepped to one of these, then called, "Mr. Morgan!" who was already on his way over crunching glass with each hurried step.

Toland left his window and came back with a pair of binoculars from under the captain's shredded leather chair and began trying to spot the flagship *Pennsylvania* through the dense heat and black smoke coming up from what was left of the stricken *Arizona.*

Morgan, still looking through his open window, began speaking in his phones. "Engine room! What is your condition, what is the pressure in number-one and two boiler rooms at this time? Can we get underway! —We have to! —Signal bridge, signal bridge!"

The reason was plain and simple. A fire was raging on *Nevada*'s bow caused by the great explosion, and it was about to be intensified with a sheet of burning oil spreading down from *Arizona*'s inferno dead ahead.

143

"The signal bridge doesn't answer, Chief. Can you make out *Pennsylvania's* hoist?"

"Yes, sir, she still reads, top to bottom—pennant zero—tack—emerg—deploy, end of hoist. That's it, sir. All ships get underway!"

Morgan was talking faster now, "I wouldn't give a damn if she read—listen, Chief, did you know that Toby—"

"Yes, I know, about 0600. I recommend we light off the gyro, but we'll have to go out magnetic till she settles down." Toland thought of mentioning his shower, but decided better of it.

"Right!" Then turning to his phones Morgan commanded, "Engine room, engine room, get an electrician to cut the gyro in."

Then like jackals coming in to torment their wounded prey, strafing planes came swooping down, machine-gunning everything in the harbor, selecting targets at random. Everyone hit the deck again just as a crackling burst of slugs passed through the starboard overhead, and on out the port bulkheads and open hatch. Again no one on the bridge was hit, and again the decks rattled as *Nevada's* angry antiaircraft batteries fired back in defiance.

But somewhere on *Nevada* somebody was getting it, Toland thought, then said aloud, "Jimmy, Mick! As soon as these bastards ease up again start checking out the engine-order-telegraph and wheel, and get the bearing circles in place. Sullivan! Have you got that tide worked out yet?"

"Yeah, Chief, she's on an ebb. Max current one point two knots at 0954." The machine-gunning stopped.

"That's good, Sully, that's good. OK, now, let's start checking things out," he said, standing straight up, "and let's clean this wheelhouse up a little." Then turning to Morgan, "You'll be going out with the current, sir."

"No, Chief! You'll be going out with the current. You'll have to do it," Morgan said, holding his phones up from his chest, "I got a whole battleship and a thousand men to take care of here. All you got to do is move us out. Understand?" Then he added, "But I'll help you when I can."

Chief Toland hesitated, then said, "Yes, sir."

Lieutenant Commander Morgan began talking again, but not to Toland. He spoke alternately through the phones, then to his recorder who worked over a clipboard full of scrap paper and holding up a cutaway configuration of *Nevada*'s hull shape, showing all voids and compartments to Morgan who would erase or color in various sections that indicated fire or flooding was under control, or not under control. "Get thirty men to the mess decks on the double, get that fire out! Block off compartment Fox 14, and flood 15!—I don't care how many men are in there, seal it off, now!—All right, fifteen seconds, no more, then seal it! We've got to keep ballast as well as watertight integrity. Keep hosing down the forward magazines, but not too heavy. I want a boiler report from number-one and two fire rooms. And keep working on that blaze at the bow."

Moving away from this busy Reserve officer who was in full command of himself and his ship, Toland turned to observe and acknowledge his own small crew.

"All checked out, Chief!" Sullivan said, his hands still on the engine-order-telegraph.

"And ready to move out," stated Mickey, facing the big ship's wheel, adding, "We can get shot at just as easy underway as moored to this sandspit."

"We heard what Mr. Morgan said to you, Chief," Jimmy smiled, but didn't say any more.

Toland looked around the battered room; a pile of debris was now in place under the chart table. He glanced at the deck clock, still ticking away at 0855. It seemed fantastic, so short a time had gone by. But then again it seemed like breakfast and coffee with his friend Charlie Mace took place years ago, if it had ever happened at all. In any case, the whole United States Navy and everything else had passed completely from one kind of world and into a totally different one in just an hour's time. Nothing and no one would ever be the same again.

Then he clinched his jaw. He knew Mickey's logic was incorrect. A moving battleship in Pearl Harbor, probably the only one, would be a choice target and an enviable kill to those flying around above. They would zero in with everything they had left. "God, what a way to go. But it's as good as any," he thought. But maybe Mickey did have a point. Look what happened to the *Oklahoma* and *Arizona,* and they were tied up. He decided to keep his thoughts to himself.

"OK, Chief, we got the power," Morgan hollered in from the port wing. "Let's get going! Take her right on out of the harbor."

"Well, Mickey, you like the movies. Somebody's bound to get a shot at this," Toland said, adjusting his head set. "Get your phones back on sailors, and get 'back to your stations. And get those life jackets on, tie 'em all the way up. Sullivan, you stand by the engine-order."

Then the chief went out on the starboard wing, observed the hawse lines and the distance to the mooring posts, and said to Jimmy, "You let me know when we are clear of everything. Lines, buoys, floating fire, and about how close we are to passing those other wagons." After Jimmy's nod Toland took one more look around, spotted the Officers' Landing astern, then headed for the port side, saying to Sullivan on the way, "Put the rudder amidship!"

Reaching the port wing, he said to Morgan, "Tell the main deck to cast off all lines, Sir!" Then to Mickey, "We want to keep it clear out here Mick. Just tell me when anything approaches or gets in our way."

Back inside Toland said, "Port back one!" Then he made for the middle ladder going down inside the ship and came back with a battle-ax.

"Engine room answers port back one, Chief!" Sullivan shouted.

"All stop!" the chief quartermaster hollered out as he began chopping away at each of the forward windows in front of the ship's wheel.

"Engine room answers all stop, Chief!" Everyone aboard felt the ship moving a little, and a mild cheer went up outside.

"Starb'd ahead two, port ahead one!" Toland said, discarding the ax in the corner then gripping the wheel and moving it to left standard rudder.

"All lines are cast off except the spring," Morgan hollered in, "and I've got axes on it now." Then back into his phones, "—Tell Stuckey to use his own best judgment!"

"Engine room answers up starb'd ahead two, port ahead one!" said Sullivan.

"You're all clear now, Chief. —Underway! All lines cast off!" *Nevada* shuddered as her screws began churning up tons of water in an effort to stop her stern way and send her forward.

"We're still going back," came Jimmy's voice through the phones, "and we're going to hit the Officers Landing. —Now!"

A wild cheer came up from the starboard side, but Toland didn't change his orders. The sound of bending and cracking wood was loud and clear; then the 32,000-ton ship began moving forward.

"All ahead two!" Toland ordered.

"Encyclopedia! You son-of-a-bitch! You always get the good side," Mickey hollered through his phones. "What does it look like, did we really smash it?"

"Engine room answers up, all ahead two, Chief!" Sullivan said.

"To smithereens!" Jimmy came back, authoritatively.

"Knock it off! And stand alert out there," Toland commanded through his phones, as he began easing his helm to midship. Then, reaching up, he pulled the brass handle above his head and made one prolonged blast of *Nevada*'s whistle that could have been heard all the way to Honolulu.

"Request permission to make eight bells on time, Sir!" Sullivan asked gleefully.

"You're about an hour late now sailor. Make it so!" Toland answered as he moved the rudder five degrees to the right bringing the ship into midchannel. Sullivan left his station just long enough to strike smartly the eight overdue bells.

The mild breeze mixed with oil smoke filtering in through the open windows nevertheless had a cooling effect on Toland's perspiring face. He wheeled the rudder back to midship and cautiously decided to reduce the engine speed to one-third as *Nevada* drew closer to the mangled hulk of *Arizona*'s charred port quarter. It was plain at a glance that no one left aboard was alive.

"All ahead one!" Toland called to Sullivan, who was now back at his post and leaning forward on the engine-order-telegraph and trying to get a good view of the burning *Arizona*, first through the open starboard windows, and then through the open hatch.

"Engine room answers all ahead one!" Sullivan answered somberly.

"There's a couple guys swimming around out here, Chief!" said Jimmy excitedly through his phones. "The main deck is throwing out some lines. We got 'em! They must have been blown off the *Arizona*."

"OK, we're moving ahead about five or six knots now. Keep your eyes and ears open. Keep lettin' me know what's going on around us," Toland said through his phones. "How is the fire on the bow, have they got it under control yet?"

"No, Chief," came Mickey's voice. "Honest to God, I think it's getting worse. The wind's fanning it up!"

Toland's heart sank a little. He knew *Nevada* couldn't go far with a fire raging on her bow, but at least they had brought the great ship away from the burning oil. Then he wondered how long it would be before their tormentors aloft would spot them and begin diving on *Nevada* again.

Now they were passing, first two by two, the five remaining battleships along the eastern side of Ford Island. And they were the first closeup witnesses of what can be done by a single well-planned surprise air attack to a whole mighty battleship division, in just an hour's time.

First in view to go by *Nevada*'s starboard side and open hatch, *West Virginia*, her main and second decks awash, sunk beside *Tennessee* inboard. Both ships had visibly taken a terrible beating. Torn, smoking holes pocked their upper decks and superstructures, where bombs and machine-gun damage had been felt moments earlier. Large quantities of threatening oil was spilling out from gaping torpedo wounds below the waterline of *West Virginia* that would for more than a generation change the once clear green waters of Pearl Harbor to a murky brown. Men were loading stretchers or running with them; others appeared standing by or working over their 5-inch AA gun mounts. But most men aboard the battered ships stopped whatever they were doing and roundly began cheering *Nevada*'s movement, and seeing what may have been to them something like 'their man' getting back into the ring after having been knocked over the ropes before the real fight had begun.

Just as *Nevada*'s flaming bow came abeam of the capsized *Oklahoma*, a Jap plane roared by *Nevada*'s port side. Five-inchers and machine guns fired back, but too late to get a hit.

"I didn't even see him coming, Chief, he came in so fast!" cried Mickey's voice, sounding a little tired this time.

"Mick, that's OK! Just give me a bearing on the signal tower, now!"

"OK, she bears—205." Then, "Chief! Here comes a whole string of them!"

Ear-shattering reports cracked from *Maryland* as she began firing in front of, then over the upturned belly of *Oklahoma* beside her, and over *Nevada*'s moving structure. It almost seemed that *Maryland* was firing right at *Nevada*, all in a mad protection of her dead mate lying next to her. Toland threaded the needle by wheeling his ship around the Ford Island dredge in the center of the channel. Bursts of machine-gun fire from the oncoming planes began striking the water in front of *Nevada* and continued a tattoo on up her port side, silencing some of her gun crew. Other crews continued firing, bagging one of the five as they went by.

Two more such passes were made but at different angles. *California*, tied to Ford Island's southernmost mooring buoys, smoking and listing heavily to port from several torpedo strikes, was also sending up volleys of antiaircraft fire. Then, the air was still and the firing stopped. It meant to Toland that high-level bombing would soon commence. Those in every enemy plane aloft, including their based aircraft carriers, must have known by now of *Nevada*'s movement and dash for the open sea.

But now, *Nevada* was bearing down on YPO Peninsula, the green finger of land marking the entrance to West Lock. And through the port windows, Hospital Point and a portion of the harbor entrance coming into view. Toland would have to make the turn to sea in about three minutes. He asked for another bridge headcount during the short reprieve in the fighting.

"I'm OK," came Jimmy's voice. "There are guys running on top of the *Oklahoma*'s bottom. You should see it, Chief."

"All right, Jimmy. Mickey, how's Mr. Morgan? —Mickey, answer up!" Toland shouted.

"Chief! I'm OK," called Morgan from around the port hatch, "but I've lost my recorder, and Harris is over in the corner passed out or in shock. What do you need!"

"I need a turn bearing on Hickam Tower. Give me a mark when the tower bears 155 true. The gyro has settled," Toland shouted.

Morgan gave a thumb up and went back to his phones strapped around his neck. At that moment the whine and scream of aerial bombs was clearly heard. Toland shouted for everybody, "Inside!" Jimmy hurried in and got next to the chart table, Sullivan left the engine-order-telegraph, announcing he was going after his buddy, "Mick!" Toland motioned for him to hurry. Explosions sounded, then two geysers of salt water shot up from the port side with the first bombs—a near miss. Drenching wet, Morgan and Sullivan came in with Mickey between them, obviously dazed and in shock. Toland knew it must be time to turn, considering advance and transfer.

"I'll get the bearing, Chief," shouted Sullivan, "155 on the Hickam Tower!"

Screams in the air meant more bombs were coming. Toland reached to stop him with his left hand, his right hand bringing the wheel to left standard rudder. It was too late. Sullivan was more than halfway through the open hatch when the first bomb struck the port bridge wing. He shot back through in mid air like a charred, old Raggedy Ann doll someone had thrown into the wheelhouse. His flying body grazed Toland's left shoulder and continued on until it landed in a heap of broken bones and flesh near his shocked friend he had just brought in to safety. Other bombs were striking aft of the wheelhouse.

Morgan, forced to concentrate on his phones again, made his way back out through the vulnerable port hatch for his configuration board. Jimmy, feeling almost useless, quickly removed his phones and decided on his own to help Morgan. The lieutenant commander called over his set for corpsmen and a couple of reliefs to make it to the bridge on the double.

The battleship, still in its turn to port, passing red channel buoy Twenty and fast coming up on the last channel course of 180 degrees leading to the harbor entrance, was only one and a half miles from the open sea.

Toland, easing the helm and alone in the wheelhouse now except for Mickey Harris wearing a blank stare and sitting near the body of his friend, sensed *Nevada* was much lower at the bow than she should be. He was glancing up at the 'pitch arm' when Slaughter, the signalman striker, bounded through the starboard hatch shouting, "Chief! The tower just sent over by light, 'Do not block harbor entrance, do not block harbor entrance!' " And while looking around, "They're all dead on the signal bridge, too."

"Well, we're not all dead down here yet, sailor!" Then, commenting on Slaughter's message, "Are you sure that's what the tower sent? I thought you couldn't read light so good."

"I can read it good enough now. I'm telling you that's what they sent. They sent it twice. 'Do not—' "

"OK, give it to Mr. Morgan. He's on the port wing."

Toland, realizing the hopelessness of the situation, was almost in relief at the new command. He didn't wait for any more commands, and said aloud to himself, "Left full rudder! Left full rudder it is, sir!" and he swung the great mahogany-rimmed wheel to port. "All back full," he said, continuing to give orders to himself, then reaching over and pulling back the two brass arms of the engine-order-telegraph and pushing them forward, then back again, stopping at red back full. The little bells inside immediately sounded. And Toland said aloud again to himself, "Engine room answers, all back full, sir!"

Morgan, back inside now with Slaughter and Jimmy behind him, called out, "Beach her, Chief! We've got to beach her, now!"

"Aye, aye, sir! The beach is dead ahead now, sir!" answered Toland with a voice hardly his own. Holding the wheel hard over to port, he watched *Nevada*'s burning nose bearing down on Hospital Point.

Unknown by Toland, Stuckey, on the main deck and busy amidship with everything from moving stretcher bearers undercover to handling ammo and directing fire fighters, had seen the inevitable beaching of his ship coming up. Taking a man with him, he ran forward to the anchor windlass above the chain locker to stand by the 'hook.' At that moment, high-level bombers at eight thousand feet began dropping another load on their choice, moving target below. The first pattern of bombs landed harmlessly in the water, missing the turning ship. Part of the second load did not miss. One bomb hit and exploded just a few feet away from the anchor windlass. Neither Chief Stuckey nor his man were even seen or heard from again.

CHAPTER XI

"PUT THE STRETCHER DOWN, MAC. I TELL YA HE MOVED!"

Still in a swing to port, her engines in full reverse causing her great propellers to grab up tons of water far below, *Nevada* began to shudder around them while heeling eight degrees to starboard. She nevertheless continued moving forward toward Hospital Point as her fantail, in a circle, was carried down the channel by the swift, ebbing current.

"It's no good, Chief! If we beach here we'll be sticking out too far in the channel," Morgan shouted as he determined the situation through the windows. "But if we could make it back over to YPO Peninsula!"

Toland spun the helm to midship putting a check on *Nevada*'s swing. She was now almost in a reversed position, heading back up the channel, still making headway but at a reducing speed and unable to avoid contact with the small portion of sandy beach in front of her.

Nevada's contact with Hospital Point was only slight and momentary, her ram bow refusing to penetrate the sand more than a few feet. With her engines still in full reverse she stopped, then withdrew so gently that most of her crew were unaware of the first grounding.

"All stop!" Toland commanded, now wheeling the rudder to starboard. The three men standing near the windows shook free of their fixed gaze in front of them and rushed for the engine-order-telegraph. Slaughter reached the brass arms first and rang up the signal to the engineers below.

"All ahead two! All ahead standard! Come on, honey, just five more minutes," Toland said, feeling the ship beginning to move forward again, this time against the current. He brought the helm to left standard, and *Nevada* cleared Hospital Point by fifteen yards.

Morgan, back at the open windows and sending commands through his phones mostly in reference to the fire still raging on the bow, pointed to an, as yet, unnamed spit of land protruding out from the peninsula across the channel. "There, right in there, Chief! That sugarcane's far enough back where it won't catch fire."

In time this spit of land, acted upon by the Territory of Hawaii Legislature and with approval of the Sovereign State of Nevada and the United States Congress, would be forever known and charted as 'Nevada Point.'

Meanwhile, with Slaughter standing by the engine-order-telegraph and Morgan pointing the way, Toland had *Nevada* aimed on her final six hundred yards' journey of the day. On the deck near the chart table Jimmy was trying to comfort his incoherent shipmate, Mickey, who was speaking mournfully.

"Come on, Sully. You got the next watch. Get your ass up now!" Mickey cried over his dead friend.

"I'll take his watch, Mick," said Jimmy. "Let him sleep, OK?"

"The hell with you, Encyclopedia!" snapped Mickey, shaking off Jimmys' hand from his shoulder. "We're the best QM Thirds in the whole world, ain't we, Sully. Hey, Sully, how's your tennis! Ain't my racket neither. And we're all teed off at golf, ain't we! How about bowlin'! Come on, man. How about bowlin'?"

"All stop!" Toland commanded, judging the distance from the bow to the sandy beach ahead.

"Engines answer, all stop!" said Slaughter.

'This time,' Toland thought, 'got to get in the sand deep enough where no current will pull her off. But not so hard that her bow will be crushed either.' "All back one! —All back two!"

Morgan, now observing the truth of the next few moments, pressed down on the little button on the mouthpiece in front of him, "All stations, all stations, prepare for collision! Prepare for collision!"

Nevada shuddered again, her engines reversing in an effort to slow down the inevitable impact. Morgan rushed over and leaned on the claxon toggle that announced the collision alarm throughout the ship. He continued shouting, "All stations, prepare for collision," right up to the moment of impact.

The surging weight of more than 32,000 tons brought against a hardly giving land mass was tremendous. The reversing engines had probably reduced the ship's speed from seven down to four knots. Everything and everyone that wasn't securely tied down, braced, or holding on to something stable, moved forward. Dishes crashed through the wardrooms, lightly secured lockers tumbled in their compartments, whale boats and launches strained or broke at their davits. Men slipped over wet or oily decks, some gun crews fell from their stations, and recently used brass 5-inch shell casings came clanking and clattering down from the upper decks. Some went bouncing over the side and splashing far below into the shallow water between *Nevada* and the beach.

Back up in the bridge area, navigation books tumbled from their cases, and Sullivan's lifeless body took another short journey, sliding across the deck like a discarded puppet and landing in a heap with several noisy helmets beneath the open pilothouse windows. Jimmy, lying flat on the deck, held on to a corner of the chart table with one arm and held tightly to his friend Mickey with his other.

Morgan braced himself against the open port hatch while Slaughter secured his two arms around the base of the engine-order-telegraph. Toland simply held onto the big wheel in front of him.

For a few long moments everyone in the wheelhouse continued holding on to whatever he had, even after the battleship came to rest. Then Toland reached over and set the two arms of the EOT to 'stop'. The little bells inside answered for the last time and *Nevada*, with a two-degree list to port, was finally still.

After scanning the skies and taking a long look around the harbor, Morgan stepped back in to announce wearily, "It's over! The attack is over, for now anyway. There's a firefighting tug heading for our bow, and the *Phoenix* and *St. Louis* and a few 'cans' are on their way to sea." Walking closer to Toland, Morgan continued, "I'm glad we weren't in their way, Chief. We could have really bottled things up around here. And anyway, I don't think we would've stayed afloat past the first sea buoy. What I'm wondering about now is, have we made complete fools of ourselves?"

"We'll know soon enough, sir," Toland answered, observing a group of people gathering on the sandy beach in front of them and growing in numbers each moment.

A tattered Second Class Yeoman and two tired-looking officers came into the wheelhouse from the port wing. One officer relieved Morgan of his phones while the other swapped vital ship's information with him. Slaughter saw in the yeoman a good recorder, and they departed for the signal bridge above.

Toland walked over to Jimmy and Mickey and knelt down with them, saying to Jimmy, "The corpsmen are on the way up now, son. If you want to, you can—"

"That's OK, Chief. If there's nothing else you want me to do, I'd like to stay with the Mick. Maybe I'll be there when he comes out of it."

Toland continued looking at him a moment, then said, holding out his hand to the young man, "You did a fine job today, Jimmy. A real fine job!"

"Thanks, Chief. But it was you and Mr. Morgan all the way. You know that!" he answered warmly, taking Toland's hand.

"You were smarter than all of us, and that's what I know!"

Jimmy's eyes reddened, and he closed them tight, but some tears squeezed out at the corners anyway, as he brought his dirty blue shirt sleeve across his pimply face.

Two corpsmen came up from the center hatch and got busy with Mickey and Sullivan. Toland rose and decided to check on his friend Charlie Mace who would be on the next deck below.

The radio room was a shambles, but most startling was a view of the burning harbor through a large jagged hole where the radio room's starboard bulkhead once was. Several people were moving in and out, and a few operators were still sitting before their typewriters copying code. Toland stopped a Third Class carrying a clipboard full of undelivered messages.

"Mace! Where's Chief Mace!"

"He's dead. Under that canvas over there. I got to go, Chief. The Japs are bombing Manila and Clark Field, and invading the Philippines right now."

Toland let him go, walked over, and stood looking down at the motionless covering. He clinched his jaw, then stooped to pull back a corner.

"I wouldn't do that, Chief," said Standsbery, Mace's First Class Radioman. "He's not all there, and he looks pretty bad. There are two other guys under there with him."

Toland looked up at Standsbery. Then, ignoring him, pulled back a corner of the canvas for a moment, then replaced it.

"It was that first bomb, Chief. It couldn't have been more than five minutes after GQ went. Fisher, Scott, and Chief Mace. Tore out that whole bulkhead over there," he said, pointing to the view of the harbor.

Raising back up, Toland sensed Standsbery would come apart if he kept talking.

"You better get back to your other radiomen. You're in charge here, you know!"

"Yeah, Chief. But what the hell happened here anyway? What the hell is going on?"

"Today we went to war, that's what's going on," the chief answered. "And you better keep your messages flowing."

Now, in a better frame of mind, he took the chief's advice and moved authoritatively back among his men.

Toland glanced down once more at the rumpled canvas form, then moved to the torn-away bulkhead and the view of the smoking harbor. The fireboat had the blaze out at the bow; several destroyers were underway and heading out of the harbor in a futile search for the Japanese carrier task force. And there were a number of small boats, gigs, and motor launches making for *Nevada*'s starboard quarter. Already an accommodation ladder was being lowered by *Nevada*'s bosun's mates. Coming aboard would be more corpsmen, doctors, and most of the officers who were on weekend liberty. The captain, and XO, and probably some staff officers would be on their way.

Toland wished his friend Mace was on one of those boats, coming back to his ship a little late instead of lying on the deck behind him and dead. He thought of Verna and the picnic they almost had, of what must she be doing and thinking right then. He thought of her father and of Donald. Then he thought of his own children back on the mainland, and what it all would mean to them.

And then Toland thought of Mace's family, his little girl with the sore arm and his junior high school son, and his Doris. She doesn't even know about her Charlie yet. When would she find out, and how?

'Some of those boats will be going right back to fleet landing', Toland thought, as he turned and hurried out, then down the three flights of ladders and on through officers' country to the mess decks below. He passed busy sailors coming and going in either direction, some with bandaged heads, arms, or legs, others with no bandages, but all glad to be alive. In the mess decks every table was folded out, and each had the more seriously wounded officers and enlisted men on top waiting for treatment. Some were beyond waiting. The less seriously wounded were sitting on the decks resting their backs against the bulkheads. Some had much to talk about, their recent terrifying or funny experiences. Others, in shock, had nothing to talk about at all. Toland spotted Ensign Lord sitting on the deck staring glassy-eyed at his feet in front of him.

"Keep moving! Keep these aisles clear!" shouted Chief Simpson. "If there is nothing wrong with you, keep the hell out of here. That's right, sailor, you too. Talk to your buddy later. You corpsmen, don't give out none of that morphine without my say-so. —Earl! How did it go for you up there. I thought we were going out to meet the whole Jap Navy for a while!"

"Well, we changed our minds. We figured they would outrun us," Toland answered. Then seriously, "There's a lot of boats lying off our fantail."

"I know, and plenty of doctors and fresh corpsmen from the beach. See you later."

Toland hurried on through the bloody activity of the crews' mess decks, and on aft along the passageways leading to the fantail, stepping over a mile or so of firehoses leading down into every compartment along the way.

"—Hey, Chief! Somebody! Give me a hand!"

Toland stopped and looked around, then ran back to the ladder he just passed. The compartment below was dark, but he could make out the figure of a man knee deep in water trying to get a hatch open. Toland looked aft at the bright opening leading onto the fantail, then back to the struggling man in the murky compartment below. Then he rode the rails down and landed in the water with him.

"I got a man on the other side of this hatch, but it's dogged down too tight, and I can't get it open."

"How do you know there's a man in there?"

"I'm the duty cook, and I put him in there myself, 0630 this morning. It's the spud locker. The guy had some extra duty to work off. I didn't know this was going to happen. —Listen!" and he pounded on the hatch with his oily fist, then waited. Immediately pounding on the other side began, then stopped.

"OK!" Toland said, "But we got to get a dogging wrench. There's got to be one around here someplace. You feel along that bulkhead and I'll go along this one."

Both men pushed through the water and passed their hands up and down the bulkheads.

"That bastard, Yates. He must have dogged himself in there and went to sleep. I didn't think about him till fifteen minutes ago and thought I'd better check on him. He probably slept through the whole—hey, Chief! I got something!" Toland turned just as something floating in the water next to him brushed against his right leg. Then both men pushed back through the water and met in front of the frozen hatch again.

The cook had a two-foot length of pipe, and without any further words both men put their backs to it and pulled with all their strength at each dog handle. First the inside ones, then they worked around to the outside handles. With each handle now free, they both pulled at the hatch while the water around them tried to keep it shut. Then it gave way with Yates pushing from the other side. One would have thought the cook and Yates were father and son, they were so glad to see each other. The current around them rushed into the smaller compartment carrying with it floating debris, and the body of a dead sailor, face down.

On the fantail, activity was crowded and somewhat confused with everyone there wanting to direct or to help. Already a makeshift morgue with thirty to forty covered bodies was set up on the port side, back near the aircraft loading crane. 'Old Glory' fluttered appropriately from the flagstaff a few feet away, while two pharmacist's mates passed through the rows of rumpled corpses, attempting to identify and tag the remains. On the starboard side, stretchers with the more seriously injured to be treated at hospitals and sick bays ashore waited on deck in a loose line, with their bearers standing by to move them up for off-loading at the Quarterdeck.

The small boats circling near *Nevada*'s stern were directed one by one to come alongside the accommodation ladder, off-load their passengers, wait, then take on two to four stretchers, depending on the size of the boat. They were then ordered to make for Fleet Landing, deposit the wounded in waiting ambulances, and return to the ship for more casualties.

Most of those hurrying up the ladder and crossing the Quarterdeck at the top were ship's company officers returning from their interrupted weekend liberty. But with loyalty, devotion to service and to country deeply imbedded in every Academy man, the heartbreaking disappointment of not being aboard his ship at her most crucial hour clearly showed on their pained, determined, and somewhat embarrassed faces. Others coming aboard were a mixture of medical officers, with their black cases and accompanying pharmacist's mates, and a few equally disappointed CPOs and enlisted personnel.

The 'morgue' was growing in size and so was the line of stretcher cases. Down from the starboard weather deck two men struggled with a stretcher to the bottom of the ladder, and proceeded to carry their burden to the enlarging ranks of the dead. An argument developed between the two sailors at each end of the stretcher.

"Put the stretcher down, Mac! I tell ya he moved!"

"You're nuts, and my name ain't Mac, Mac!"

"You're name's Stupid! Now put the stretcher down!"

Before the stretcher touched the deck a doctor and pharmacist, overhearing the argument in passing, were hurriedly unstrapping the victim and found him breathing erratically, but breathing. The black bag was opened, and an operation of sorts was performed then and there. Then the two astonished sailors were directed to move the stretcher to the waiting line for the new patient's transfer to the beach with the others.

Chief Toland, his khaki cloth cap transferred from his back pocket to his head, maneuvered his way through the human traffic and knots of people on the fantail. He overheard one officer proclaiming to a small group of other officers. "And the Secretary of the Navy wants Commander Morgan to call him at his convenience."

The most commanding figure on the fantail was *Nevada's* recently returned executive officer, in his shirtsleeves, directing and channeling various personnel and attempting to keep the Quarterdeck traffic flowing as smoothly as possible. He had arrived in one of the first boats, along with the anxious captain who was now touring and inspecting his damaged ship.

A call from the XO went up to clear the fantail of all personnel not actually engaged in necessary traffic. Toland, near the head of the line of stretchers to leave the ship, walked over and relieved one of the stretcher bearers. The bandaged sailor at the chief's feet seemed familiar to Toland, and he was about to stoop down for a closer look, but was interrupted.

"Hey, Wheels!"

Toland turned to face Chief Gonza. His coat under one arm, hat pushed slightly back on his tanned forehead, had just crossed the Quarterdeck.

"I missed the show, but I bet you didn't."

Toland half smiled but didn't answer.

"I wish I hadn't been ashore," he continued truthfully. "How's the signal gang!"

"They're shot up pretty bad, I think. You have a good man in Slaughter." Then looking down at the stretcher, "I'm going to be gone about two hours. Will you take over?"

"Yeah, but I'm going to check on my signal bridge first.

163

Do you want to swap hats?"

"No, but I'll take a couple of your butts."

"Sure, take the whole pack. I got another."

"Gonza," Toland said, in an attempt to ease the pain he saw in the chief signalman's face, "I was only aboard by accident myself."

Chief Gonza smiled a little, then said, "I gotta go!"

Toland lit one of the cigarettes, and knelt beside the injured sailor in the stretcher. The boy managed a smile behind the bandages, and Toland recognized him as the mess cook who served his Sunday morning breakfast to him and Mace three or four hours earlier. Toland smiled back and offered him a drag on the cigarette, but the young man's eyes declined it.

The PA system clicked on audibly for the first time since GQ had sounded earlier in the morning.

"This is the Captain speaking. I want to express to you, to each of you, the deep concern and pride I have for *Nevada*, her officers and men this day. Those that have been aboard since early this morning, I say to you, well done. And to those who came aboard late, I will share with you the eternal regret of not participating in *Nevada's* finest hour. But there will be other days and other fine hours for *Nevada*, and at that time we will be a full crew. Thank you, carry on!"

CHAPTER XII

*"OFF-LOAD WOUNDED THIS PIER.
MOVE UP CURTISS, YOU'RE BLOCK-
ING RALEIGH!
SHOVE OFF NEVADA, YOUR BOAT'S
LOADED!"*

    With four stretchers firmly secured athwart ships for easier riding and the coxun having received his orders from the Quarterdeck, the thirty-six-foot motor launch cast off from the lower platform of *Nevada's* accommodation ladder and began the mile-and-a-half ride back up the channel, to Fleet Landing.

    To the left and right of the moving boat, Toland viewed with quiet amazement the damage and destruction given his Navy and the harbor by the gambling Japanese marauders. It was severe, and the loss of life when tallied would present a staggering figure for the Navy. But it was not total destruction, or annihilation. Warships, mostly destroyer types, were getting underway and leaving the harbor to search Hawaiian waters for the enemy or join up with Halsey's task force returning from Midway. Wherever there was fire there were plenty of men trying to put it out. Wherever there was destruction there were plenty of men trying to repair it. Already teams of divers and salvage personnel were on their way, or on the scene of every stricken vessel in the harbor. Most notably, *Oklahoma's* bottom, now facing the noonday sun, had a swarm of rescuers tapping and cutting into her hull to save what lives they could.

    On rounding the north corner of Ten-Ten Dock for the

approach to Fleet Landing at the far end of Southeast Lock, Toland optimistically drew two probable conclusions: one, the Navy, although badly crippled, was still a fighting Navy. And two, Pearl Harbor although shot up in various places, was still a good Navy base. The Japanese had succeeded in destroying and sending several ships to the bottom, but she failed in any concentrated effort to destroy the Shipyard, the means on which any Navy depends for maintenance and repair. The dry docks were still intact; the Baker Docks with their cranes and equipment seemed hardly touched. And across from the Shipyard, the Sub base and several submarines looking ready as ever.

'We still got a Navy and we still got a base,' Toland thought, as the first line went over on the floating pier marked 'Dog'. The coxun had obeyed the hurriedly hand-lettered sign tacked up on the pier post that read OFF LOAD WOUNDED THIS PIER. Several boats were alongside, their personnel engaged in that business.

Picking up his end of the stretcher, Toland guessed at two more probabilities. It was the end of the battleship era. Morgan was right, and Brock's premonition was true. No more would countries depend on these big lumbering hulks as their first line of defence. Carriers, that's what they would depend on now, the Japanese had seen to that this day. And, looking down at the injured sailor in front of him, this day the Japs had managed to get the whole U.S. Navy mad at them.

"Are you coming right back?" the coxun shouted. "I can't wait on you, Chief."

"I'll be taking the next boat. Wait five minutes on these other bearers, then shove off!"

"Five minutes, aye!"

Fleet Landing was a beehive of activity. The duty Shore Patrol was having a time of it trying to keep order and assist the men. Overhead loudspeakers were continuously blaring out orders, "*California*! Make port side 'Able'.

Curtiss boat, last call. *Raleigh!* Make starboard side 'Charlie'. Shove off *Maryland,* your boat's loaded. *Curtiss,* shove off! *Dobbin* whaleboat Move up, you're blocking *Raleigh.*"

There was no shoving or pushing, but several hundred anxious sailors of every rank and rate were trying to get back aboard their ships, or trying to learn the fate of them. A large group of bewildered sailors, having already learned the worst about their ships, were just sitting on the ground discussing what they should do next.

Waiting corpsmen now escorted *Nevada's* stretchers past a line of various types of vehicles doubling as ambulances, and stopped at a dusty yellow school bus with engines warmed up and the driver ready to go. Two other stretchers were on the deck at the far end of the bus.

"Where you going with these guys?" Toland inquired of the corpsman supervising the placement of *Nevada's* injured.

"Naval Hospital, Aiea."

After directing the other bearers to return to the waiting boat, Toland asked the driver to drop him off at the Main Gate, then kneeled down in the middle of the aisle with his burden of the past half hour.

"I'll come by to see you in a couple of days, buddy." Then, glancing again at the tag tied to the side of his stretcher, he said, "What's your folks call you, Bob or Robert? I'll bet they call you Robert!"

Toland continued making small talk with the young man who only smiled in return as the bus rumbled along the gravel road, the driver sounding his horn most of the way. Then with his foot coming down easy on the brakes he said, "Main Gate, Chief."

The bus never came to a full stop, just slowed down long enough to let the chief jump clear and into the anxious crowd around the open Main Gate.

Again there was no pushing or panic, but the Shore Patrol at this post had the additional job of trying to comfort the anxious civilians that had grown to a mass of several thousand on the other side of the cyclone fence, with their endless pleading questions of news of this or that ship. Most people seemed content just to stare through the fence and wait, while others, desiring to help in some way, told each other to keep back, to keep the way clear for the servicemen to come and go, and to open a path for the buses and ambulances and other vehicles.

Even in wash khakis and cloth cap Toland had no difficulty passing through the Main Gate. The enemy was more distinguishable on this side of the world than on the European side. Not just because he had made the war, but the way he made it. His years of expansion and conquest had already brought the short Oriental under suspicion and distrust from his neighbors throughout Southeast Asia and the West. Now it was complete hostility. He had inadvertently made brothers and sisters out of all those who were not of his stature and likeness. But many innocent and loyal Americans of Japanese descent would feel this hostility. And many a short Filipino or Chinese ally would have to go through the pangs of incrimination until his identity was established.

Passing through the crowd that politely gave way to the chief, as he hurriedly made his way to the parking lot, Toland couldn't help but notice the divergence of people as faces were casting pleading, questioning, sometimes compassionate glances in his direction. Men, women, young and old, prostitutes to preachers, well-dressed and some not so well-dressed. Some, even in housecoats and pajamas. Some ventured their questions.

"—Chief, can you tell me about the *Oglala?*"

"I can't say, sir."

"Is it true the *Arizona's* gone, and the *Oklahoma,* too?"

"They were hit, ma'am."

"—I have a son on the *West Virginia!*"

"I'm off the *Nevada*, sir."

"—*Nevada!* Was the *Nevada* sunk?"

"No, ma'am. She's aground but not sunk."

"—Thank God!"

Continuing to avoid conversations and direct answers, Toland finally found himself alone in the CPO section of the lot, and had no trouble locating Mace's gray '34 Studebaker. Now, behind the wheel of the stuffy car, he rolled down the window, noticed a book of matches on the dash left by his friend, lit one more of Gonza's cigarettes, then reached under the seat, felt around on the floor, and came up with the keys.

After inching his way in low gear back through the yellow dust and the crowds of people, he moved onto the highway leading into town. Toland passed several cars stalled on the side and still more people, and was about to shift into second but jammed on the brakes instead to avoid hitting a tall, well-built Naval officer who had just stepped from the crowd to the middle of the road, both arms flagging down the Studebaker.

Opening the right-hand door himself and getting in without waiting for any response from Toland, he said, "These damn people! Give me a lift into town, Chief."

"I'm not going all the way in, but I'll take you as far as I'm going."

"How far ya going?"

"I'll take you as far as the Punch Bowl, then I'm cutting across the Pali to Kaneohe Village."

The young officer thought a moment, then said, "OK."

Toland continued driving through the canefields and lowlands for a mile or so and made no conversation with his companion.

"Good God, wasn't that something though!" the officer began. "All those planes and bombing in the harbor. I thought it was a practice attack staged by the Army or something. I'm in the Administration Building, Duty Officer today of all days, but just until noon. My wife was supposed to pick me up. No wife, no car, and no phone. They're all busy. She's probably worried sick about me."

He waited a moment for some reply, then said, "I'll bet your friend and mine, Roosevelt, had something to do with this." He pronounced the first syllable in the president's name as in 'rooster'.

The Studebaker bounced up and down and swayed from side to side along the unpaved road, dodging other vehicles from time to time. Toland took his eyes off the road just long enough to stare back at the conversationalist for a moment.

Another half mile went by, and then the road became paved. On the northwest end of Honolulu fire trucks and clusters of people were gathered around a smoking home or vacant lot here and there. The anxious officer beside the chief became visibly worried.

"Listen, Chief! Koko Head, that's where I live. It's only fifteen minutes from here, what do ya say!"

Toland glanced at the gas gauge. It was less than a quarter full but he was about to say 'all right', then the fine-looking officer made one more comment.

"I could order you to, you know. Commandeer this heap, as they say."

Toland drove one more half-block to the intersection of King Street and Punch Bowl, applied the brakes a little harder than necessary, reached over, and opened the passenger's door.

"I wouldn't do that, sir," the chief said politely. "This is where I turn, sir!"

The officer's face reddened. He hesitated a moment, then got out and slammed the door a lot harder than necessary.

Toland kept the old Studebaker in second gear for most of the eight-mile drive, up the Pali and on down to Kaneohe. At the summit he noticed several smoke columns moving skyward in various direction around the island but not as black and billowy as before. And one was moving up in the direction he was heading, and that could only have been the Navy Sea Plane Base at Kaneohe Bay.

Maybe he shouldn't be doing this, he thought while turning the corner onto his friend's street and driving down into the valley of little wooden frame houses. Several children were already out playing in the street, seemingly unconcerned of the morning's events. But yet it might be days before she learned the truth about her husband. And too, he wasn't kidding himself, he was anxious to see Verna—to know that she was all right, and for her to know that he was all right. Right or wrong he had done it now, he was here.

But he couldn't stay long, he told himself as the Studebaker came to rest in Mace's driveway.

Little Cathy seemed to appear from nowhere, and landing on the running board, "Mr. Toland! See my cast?" she beamed. "Will you sign it like everybody else? I thought you were Daddy. Has he got the duty?"

"Yes, Kitten, he's got the duty," Toland answered, shutting the car door. "Is your mother inside?"

"Yes, sir, she's inside with Leon. They're listening to the radio. Please, Mr. Toland, sign my cast. I got a pencil right here!"

"OK, Honey, then you stay out and play. All right?" The white cast was getting dirty already from playing and with a dozen or so signatures from people around the neighborhood. Toland signed his name near Verna's as the screen door on the porch opened with its rusty squeal.

"Earl! Is Charlie all right?" asked Doris, with a trace of doubt in her voice.

Cathy darted off saying she was "Going to tell Verna you're here."

Inside, Toland broke the news to her standing up. She tried with her first words to be calm and detached from the shattering news, and mentioned they should all make plans to go back to Ohio and to their Aunt Ruby. Then she couldn't hold it. "-Damn Navy!" she sobbed heavily. "Who gives a damn about Charlie Mace anyway? -Who gives a damn?" And then she went into the kind of cry that is reserved only for the lost loved dead. And her son helped her into her lonely bedroom.

In a few minutes Leon came back out alone to face Toland, and Toland felt even more helpless and clumsy with his friend's son.

"She needs you a lot now. You stick by her. I'll be back to see you in a few days." Turning to open the door, and stopping halfway through, Toland looked back at the boy. He looked as though he wanted more than that from his father's friend, so Toland tried. "Your dad was somebody. A lot of people gave a lot today. A lot of dads just like yours. And a lot of people care more for your dad than just a damn. He was a chief in the United States Navy, and that's got to be something. OK, Leon?"

The boy answered, "Yes, sir."

On the brown lawn in front of Mace's house Verna was in Toland's arms. After a few long moments he said, "I can't wait. Will you drive me down to the Sea Plane Base? I can get a lift back to Pearl from there."

"No! If you have to go I'll drive you all the way," she said in a trembling voice.

"No good. It's too mixed up in town, and too many civilians around that gate now, anyway."

As they were getting into the Pontiac, Verna's father crossed the driveway toward the car.

"Chief Toland! I'm glad you're all right," the paunchy middle-aged gentleman said, his hand held out. "This kind of makes me wrong about a lot of things, doesn't it?"

"No, sir, I don't think so. Just timing, maybe. And everybody's mixed up on that today."

"My family and I want you to spend Christmas with us, if you're in the area." Then he added, feeling a loss for words, "Maybe we could get in a few games of chess, or something."

"Yes, sir, if I'm in the area."

The surf rose and pounded on the coral reef a few hundred yards off the highway as they drove along the coast heading for Mokapu Peninsula.

"It might have been a swell day for a picnic," Toland said, glancing out his side window.

"When will we ever have another picnic, ever?" was her reply in deep thought.

Toland set out lightly to convince her this was not the end of the world, only that the world was different for them and everyone else now. But conceivably they would have long absences from each other for a while.

Then he leaned forward, noticing a Navy gray bus coming out of the base gate ahead.

"I got to make that bus, honey. I'll bet it's going right back to Pearl. You go back home and sit with Doris a while. She needs another female right now."

The bus driver held his vehicle still as he watched the couple in a fast embrace in front of him.

"Earl! Oh, Earl!" she said holding onto his left hand as he tried to break away. "Did you know you went to war with your house shoes on?"

Toland looked down and smiled at himself, then back at Verna, "I'll see you later, honey. I love you!"

"Earl! Will you ever ask me to marry you?"

"Yes, ma'am!" he hollered back from the step of the bus, "On the next seventy-two. If you're still willin'!"

He waved back to her from the windows of the moving bus and said to the driver, "Pearl Harbor, Main Gate?"

"Right, Chief! You late getting back to your ship?"

"Yes, a little."

Several sailors in dungarees near the center of the bus were loudly conversing on the day's happenings. One obviously more informed than the others was trying to bring his buddies up to date.

"-Nine battleships! And one of them gets underway. It usually takes four hours for one of those babies to get up enough steam just to move from one side of the pier to the other. The *Utah*, she's on the bottom! The *Arizona*, blown higher than a kite! The *Oklahoma*, never had a chance!

And all those other wagons, dead plant. Can't move a foot. Then here she comes, proud as a peacock. Right down the middle of the channel, her bow burning like the torch on the Statue of Liberty. -The old *Nevada*, BB thirty-six. Takin' lead and pourin' it right back at 'em. God, what a sight. And listen, there weren't no officers on board!" the sailor continued, throwing his arms up in the air. "Guess who got her underway!"

"-A Second Class Bosun Mate!"

"Wrong!"

"-I heard it was a Signalman or Quartermaster!"

"Wrong again, mates. It was a Fireman and a Mess Cook!" he announced proudly and with authority.

The sailor's conversation stayed with the *Nevada* for a while longer, then shifted to other notable incidences involving other ships in the harbor that morning.

Toland, out of matches, tapped one of the listening sailors for a light, then relaxed back with another of Gonza's smokes. He wished he had had his pipe.

Toland's shoulder still ached from the blow he received earlier in the wheelhouse. He thought of Sullivan, and Brock. Both, good men. Then he remembered Pollard's remark of seeing two swimmers, possibly from the *Arizona*. Maybe Brock swam ashore, or maybe he was picked up by some other vessel. It was worth hoping for. His friend Charlie Mace was of course beyond hope, but he would always occupy a place in his thoughts. A good friend.

The concerned crowd around the Main Gate was still large but not as big as it had been earlier. The Shore Patrol guard at the gate, observing the passengers inside, waved the bus on through. The driver parked in front of the busy Administration Building. Toland, the last one out of the bus, hurriedly walked, then began running as he heard the blaring loudspeakers over at Fleet Landing announce, "-*Nevada*! Last call. *Helena*, make port side 'Charlie'! *West Virginia*, tie up astern *Tennessee*! Shove off

San Francisco, you're loaded!"

Toland ran through the gray and white wooden structure, trying to avoid bumping into other moving sailors who were trying to get back to their ships, too.

"-Shove off *Nevada!* Your boat's loaded!"

Toland, running down the ramp onto the floating pier heard, "Come on, Chief!"

He grabbed the side of the backing-down boat and pulled himself over the gunwhales. He made it.

Nevada did indeed have another day and other fine hours, as did each of the other remaining five old battleships.

Within the year 1942, as needed, the six were raised, dry-docked, and refitted, and returned to the growing U.S. Fleet in time to participate in some of the greatest sea battles the world has ever known.

While her sisters *California, Maryland, Pennsylvania, Tennessee,* and *West Virginia* continued supporting Admiral Halsey's Third Fleet in the Pacific and Philippine Sea engagements and operations, *Nevada* was temporarily relieved. Under orders she steamed southeast for the Panama Canal, broke into the Atlantic, and arrived in time to support the Allied landings in Africa. Then turning north for the west coast of France she brought her ten 14-inch guns to bear against the German occupation of Europe and greatly assisted the Allied landings at Normandy.

Four months later and back in the Pacific, she rejoined her other sisters. Then, under Vice Admiral Kincaid's Seventh Fleet, she took part in the five-day Battle of Leyte Gulf, October 22 through October 27, 1944. This, the largest naval battle ever fought in history. Total number of warships committed to this action; 231. U.S. losses: 4 aircraft carriers, 9 destroyers, 1 high-speed transport, 7 submarines, and almost 2,800 American sailors. Japanese losses: 7 aircraft carriers, 4 battleships, 14 cruisers, 32 destroyers, 11 submarines, and more than 10,000 Japanese sailors.

It must be said that more than half of all American service personnel participating in that action were reservists.

The result of this enormous effort: General MacArthur's forces retook the Philippine Islands, and Japan was finished as a sea power.

Nevada's final act in service for the United States and the Navy was 'Ground Zero' in the first postwar atomic test blast at Bikini Atoll, July 1, 1946.

In a letter dated April 3, 1965, Fleet Admiral Chester W. Nimitz wrote to, then Chief of Naval Operations, Admiral David L. McDonald.

"–Several times in recent weeks I have been quoted, correctly, that as bad as our losses were at Pearl Harbor on 7 December 1941, they could have been devastatingly worse, had the Japanese returned for more strikes against our Naval installations, surface oil storage and our submarine base installations. Such attacks could have been made with impunity as we had little left to oppose them. Furthermore, I have been correctly quoted in saying that it was God's divine will that Kimmel did not have his Fleet at sea to intercept the Japanese Carrier Task Force that attacked P.H. on 7 December 1941. That task force had a fleet speed at least 2 knots superior to our speed, and Kimmel could not have brought the Japanese to a gun action unless they wanted it. We might have had one carrier but I doubt if the *Lexington* could have joined in time. Picture if you can, 6 Japanese carriers working on our old ships which would be without air cover, or had the Japanese wanted to avoid American air attacks from shore, they could have delayed the action until out of range of shore based aircraft. Instead of having our ships sunk in the shallow protected waters of P.H. they could have been sunk in deep water, and we could have lost all of our trained men instead of the 3,800 approx. lost at P.H. There would have been few trained men to form the nucleus of the crews for the new ships nearing completion. Not only were the ships of the enemy task force faster, they were more modern, and the Japanese main fleet under Yamamoto was in the rear, in support, if needed. Nagumo, the Commander of the P.H. Attack Force, missed a great chance by not following up his attack. . .

Warmest regards and best wishes—
C. W. NIMITZ

WALLACE LOUIS EXUM

Glossary of Nautical and Navy Terms

Azimuth . . . . . .a visual bearing of a heavenly body, i.e.,
    the sun, star
CDO . . . . .command duty officer
CO . . . . .commanding officer
DR . . . . .dead reconned
ETA . . . . .estimated time of arrival
Gee-dunk . . . . .ice cream, pudding
Grinder . . . . .practice marching area
GQ . . . . .general quarters
Jack of
the Dust . . . . . .assistant to the store keeper, cook, baker
MA . . . . .master at arms

Noon Posit . .ship's calculated position at 12 noon while
    underway
OD . . . . .officer of the deck
OPS . . . . .operations, operations department
Peloris . . . . . . .stand with bowl holding compass card or
    compass repeater
PO . . . . .petty officer
POD . . . . .plan of the day
Poggy Bait . . . . .candy
Prep . . . . .alphabet flag P. a signal, 5 minutes to col-
    ors; 8 A.M. and sunset
QM . . . . .quartermaster
Sponson
deck . . . . . . .projected out from ships side allowing grea-
    ter arc of visibility

178

Scuttlebutt drinking fountain, unconfirmed reports
Tin can ....destroyer
Wheels ....slang for quartermaster
XO ....executive officer
YPO ....Waipio Peninsula